THE MADONNA OF NOTRE DAME

ALEXIS RAGOUGNEAU

Translated by
Katherine Gregor

NEW VESSEL PRESS
NEW YORK

THE MADONNA OF NOTRE DAME

New Vessel Press

www.newvesselpress.com

First published in French in 2014 as *La Madone de Notre-Dame*
Copyright © 2014 Éditions Viviane Hamy
Translation Copyright © 2016 Katherine Gregor

Cover design: Liana Finck
Book design: Beth Steidle

Library of Congress Cataloging-in-Publication Data
Ragougneau, Alexis
[La Madone de Notre-Dame. English]
The Madonna of Notre Dame/ Alexis Ragougneau;
translation by Katherine Gregor.
p. cm.
ISBN 978-1-939931-39-9
Library of Congress Control Number 2016908534
I. France – Fiction

This novel mainly takes place in Notre Dame de Paris, hence the locations described will sound familiar both to the cathedral regulars and to occasional visitors.

However, the events and characters portrayed in this story are fictional.

THE MADONNA OF NOTRE DAME

MONDAY

"Gérard, there's a bomb alert. In the ambulatory. Serious stuff this time. Big."

His shoulder wedged in the doorway, a huge bunch of keys hanging at the end of his arm, the guard watched the sacristan fuss around, open all the sacristy cupboards, and pull out rags, sponges, silverware polish, while muttering expletives of his own composition at regular intervals.

"Gérard, are you listening? You should take a look, really. Fifteen years on the job, I've never seen anything like it. It's enough to blow up the whole cathedral."

Gérard interrupted his search and finally appeared to take an interest in the guard. The latter had just hung the keys on a single nail stuck in the sacristy paneling.

"Later on, if you like, I'll go see. Is that all right? Are you happy?"

"What's going on today, Gérard? Haven't you got time for important things anymore?"

"Look, you're starting to really piss me off. Thirty years I've been working here and it's the same thing every year: every August fifteenth they have to make a goddamn mess in the sacristy. And I can never find anything the next day. I have to spend two hours cleaning up. I don't understand why it has to be so difficult. They arrive, they put on their vestments, they do their procession and their Mass next door, they come back, they take off their vestments, and see you next year ... Why do they have to go rummaging in the cupboards?"

"Tell me, Gérard, what have you lost?"

"My gloves. My box of gloves for the silverware. If I don't have them I wreck my hands with their shitty products."

"You want me to help you look? I've got time—just finished opening up."

"Don't worry, here, found them. I don't know why it's so hard to put things back where they belong, I mean, Jesus H. Christ ..."

The guard fumbled in his pocket, inserted coins into the slit of the coffee machine, and pushed a button. He signaled good-bye to the sacristan and then, a steaming cup in his hand, started to walk back to the interior of the cathedral. Gérard caught up with him in the corridor.

"So tell me about your bomb ... Worth seeing?"

"The works, I promise: the ticktock, the time switch, and the sticks of dynamite."

"OK, I'll go see later, before the nine o'clock Mass. Might still be there. Where's your explosive device again?"

"In the ambulatory, outside the chapel of Our Lady of the Seven Sorrows. You'll see—impossible to miss."

The nave was slowly beginning to fill with its daily stream of tourists. Between eight and nine in the morning, they were mostly from the Far East: Notre Dame was the opening number on a program that would subsequently lead them, within the same day, to the Louvre, Montmartre, the Eiffel Tower, the Opéra, and the stores on Boulevard Haussmann.

Gérard pushed his cart loaded with cardboard boxes, stopping outside every side chapel. With a mechanical gesture, he would cut around the base of every box, then lift the lid, revealing a stack of candles with a picture of the Blessed Virgin Mary, which he would then immediately place in the tailor-made stands. Above the candle dispenser was written, in luminous letters and several languages: your offering is entirely up to you. The suggested donation was five euros. Then, with an equally weary gesture, he would empty the neighboring metal racks where, the previous day, several hundred candles had burned down over the course of hours, giving way to a new row of votive candles, prayers, and words of hope addressed to the Virgin Mary. A little later, another member of the staff would come and empty the collection boxes full of coins and banknotes into secure canvas sacks. There were similar stands with candles all over the cathedral, placed in strategic locations, at the base of statues, at the foot of crucifixes, in chapels devoted to private prayer. The morning promised to be a long one, and the fifteen years that stood between him and retirement a long road paved with tens of thousands of cardboard boxes, each filled with candles with a picture of the Blessed Virgin Mary.

Gérard sighed and resumed his round. Like every day for years now, Madame Pipi, invariably seated on the same chair next to the Virgin of the Pillar, invariably wearing her straw hat studded with red plastic flowers, invariably gave him a panic-stricken look and opened her mouth to say something to him. Like every day for years now, Madame Pipi thought better of it and, by way of conversation, crossed herself. With a little luck, she'd leave Gérard the morning free to complete his round. Then, invariably, the crazy old woman would end up falling asleep, and let a trickle of urine escape from under her, which would then have to be wiped away with a floor cloth.

A little farther, he greeted two cleaning women who were finishing sweeping the north transept, hushed a group of Chinese tourists whose cackling echoed through the cathedral, which was otherwise still quiet at that time, then, pushing his cart, set off along the black and white tiled floor of the ambulatory. That's when his colleague, the guard, came to mind. Immediately, he saw her. Or rather, in the half light, he just made her out.

The bombshell was indeed there, at the very end of the ambulatory, perfectly still, alone, as though delicately placed on the bench outside the chapel of Our Lady of the Seven Sorrows. Gérard approached and started emptying the nearest candle rack. The few candles lit by the first visitors of the day spread more shadow than light, so that what he was able to distinguish was a form rather than a body, a profile rather than a face. She was wearing a short white dress made of such sheer fabric it followed closely every curve, every bend in her flesh. Her black hair, shimmering in places, cascaded over her neck and shoulders like a river of silk. Her hands, joined in prayer like those of a child, rested on her bare thighs. On her feet, held demurely together under the bench like those of a schoolgirl, she had a pair of high-heeled pumps so white and varnished that it was futile to resist a glance. They underlined her slender ankles and the contours of her calves.

Gérard lost himself in the contemplation of this stunning figure, forgetting for a moment his boxes of candles, his cart, his hassles, and the monotony of his work as sacristan. However, he was soon interrupted by the crackle of a radio, the one he wore at his belt, emitting his name.

"Guard to sacristan ... Gérard? ... Gérard, do you read me?"

"Yes, I can hear you. What do you want?"

"Did you go look?"

"I'm right here."

"Is she still there?"

"Yes. Good as gold."

"And?"

"Definitely explosive ... You were right."

He put back his walkie-talkie with the guard's laughter still resounding from it, then, somewhat reluctantly, finished cleaning out the candle rack. Behind him, a handful of worshippers were already entering the chancel, where the nine o'clock Mass was about to begin. He had to get the necessary liturgical accessories ready. Father Kern was officiating this morning, and Father Kern did not tolerate delays.

A little later, he again had occasion to go through the ambulatory. An automatic dispenser of medals stamped with *Ave Maria Gratia Plena* had just become jammed and a tourist, a corpulent American woman, was tormenting the refund button. In the chancel, the Mass was following its course. Father Kern was delivering the day's homily in his metallic, authoritative voice, plunging the cathedral into a respectful silence. As he opened the cover of the medal dispenser and the jammed coins fell one by one as though from a piggy bank, Gérard ventured a glance at the young woman dressed in white. She was there, she hadn't budged, her hands still clasped together on her pale thighs, her two pumps still united. Outside, the sun was rising straight up in line with the chapel and, penetrating the stained glass in the east, was starting to bathe the young woman's translucent face in a red and blue halo worthy of a Raphael Madonna. Motionless on her bench reserved for prayer, protected by a rope that isolated her from visitors and gave her the appearance of a holy relic, she stared at the statue of the Virgin of Seven Sorrows with an oddly vacant expression.

Gérard closed the medal dispenser and took a couple of steps toward the young woman in white, but the American tourist was already ahead of him. She took a bill from her handbag and pushed it through the slit in the stand, then took four candles, which she lined up on the nearby rack before lighting them one by one. Their flickering light finally illuminated the girl's face.

The tourist crossed herself and approached the bench. In a heavily accented whisper, she asked the young woman in white if she could sit next to her in order to pray. Still motionless, the girl did not deign to reply, her eyes as though transfixed by the statue of Our Lady of the Seven Sorrows. After repeating her question and still not obtaining an answer, the American deposited her posterior on the bench, the wood groaning slightly beneath her weight. Then, as if in slow motion, as if in a nightmare from the dead of night, the white Madonna slowly nodded. Her chin came down on her chest then, gently, almost gracefully, her whole body toppled forward before collapsing on the checkered tiles.

That's when the fat American woman started to scream.

"She must have fallen on her face once the rigor mortis started wearing off. Until then, your customer was sitting on her bench nice and stiff." The medical examiner took off one of his latex gloves and scratched his head before continuing. "Shall I wait for the magistrate or get on with it right away?"

In answer to the doctor, Landard pulled a pack of Gitanes out of his jacket pocket, brought one up to his lips then, looking around, momentarily decided against lighting it. "Give her time to cross the square. Poor little thing, she may not be used to walking."

"Do we know who's on duty?"

"Yes, we know. It's the little Mistinguett."

"Who's that?"

"The little blond with the glasses. The one with the rather nice legs."

"Kauffmann?"

"That's right, Kauffmann."

"Cute, cold as a blade and stiff as the Law. None of the smooth operators at the Palais de Justice can ever get her to go out for a drink."

"Think she's a dyke?"

"Don't know. But she knows her case files inside out. And she's hardly ever late."

Like an echo to the medical examiner's assessment, the sound of quick, high-heeled footsteps reverberated in the ambulatory. The young woman walked through the small forensics team in white overalls, who were in fact waiting for the committing magistrate to arrive so that they could start work, then marched up to the tarps protecting the crime scene.

"Doctor ... Captain Landard ... Claire Kauffmann, deputy committing magistrate. What have we got?"

The doctor put his glove back on. "Very clean, almost too clean. We can start right away if you like."

The corpse was lying under the aggressive spotlights set up by the technical team. With a curt gesture, Claire Kauffmann flattened the back of her skirt over her thighs and squatted by the body. Her eyes immediately lingered on the dead woman's neck. "Strangulation?"

The medical examiner also kneeled. "Yes, the marks are quite clear. She also has a slightly raised upper lip and bruises on her forearms, look. The firefighter who first examined her noticed them immediately. He was the one who called the police at about ten this morning."

The magistrate turned to Landard, who was standing back. "Wasn't it somebody from here who called you?"

"They thought she'd fainted, and when someone faints, they call the fire department."

"Any idea who she is?"

"There's no purse, no papers, no cell phone. Absolutely nothing."

"Strange outfit to wear in a church. A bit see-through. See-through and short."

"If all the girls dressed like this for Mass, French churches would be brimming. Brimming with parishioners, I mean."

"Parishioners like you, captain?"

Landard stuffed his fists in the pockets of his jacket. The magistrate hadn't even taken the trouble to look at him. She turned away from him in a definitive gesture and went up to the medical examiner.

"Time of death, doctor?"

"I'll just take her temperature and let you know right away, madame."

Leaving the medical examiner to his thermometer, Claire Kauffmann and Captain Landard went back to the ambulatory, where Lieutenant Gombrowicz was waiting for them. Unable to bear it any longer, Landard took out a disposable lighter, shook it, and lit the cigarette that was still hanging from his lips. He inhaled deeply, blew smoke from his nostrils, and gave Gombrowicz a quizzical look. The latter pulled a notebook from the back pocket of his jeans and deciphered the first pages, which were a jungle of words, question marks, childlike sketches, and crossed out information.

"So here's the story: this morning, shortly before ten, the girl who was sitting on a bench reserved for praying suddenly fell flat on the stone floor. The cathedral called the fire department, who arrived within five minutes and recorded the death."

Claire Kauffmann interrupted Gombrowicz. "In this particular case, who is the cathedral?"

"In this particular case, them over there."

The young lieutenant turned toward a little group waiting at the other end of the ambulatory, by the entrance to the sacristy: two priests, one of whom was still wearing his mass robes, were standing on either side of a man in a light blue, short-sleeved shirt. Gombrowicz beckoned to the latter to come forward.

"He's the sacristan who picked up the deceased."

Gérard had to state his name and job title, then answer a volley of questions from the magistrate.

"You're the one who found the victim this morning?"

"That's right."

"When she fell on the floor?"

"That's right."

"And was it you who called the fire department?"

"No, that was Father Kern over there."

"Is Father Kern the tall, bald one, or the short, dark one?"

"The short, dark one. He was the one saying Mass when the girl in white fell off the bench. An American tourist started screaming, so Father Kern came out of the chancel to see what was going on."

"And had you already noticed the young woman in white?"

"She'd been there a little while."

"Had she attracted your attention?"

Gérard stuffed his hands in his pockets and hung his head. "I mean she was dressed a bit ... how can I put it?"

"In a provocative way? Is that it?"

"You could say that, yes. At the same time, there are quite a lot of miniskirts here in the summer. We gave up chasing after them ages ago. If we had to refuse to let all the girls in short dresses into the church, we'd be at it all day."

"I see."

"Some of them show up in bikini tops. Those we tell to go

away and put some clothes on. Everything's got a limit, even when it's very hot."

"Of course. We wouldn't want one of Captain Landard's parishioners to catch a nasty heat-stroke right in the middle of the cathedral, now, would we?"

The sacristan gave Landard a puzzled look. The magistrate continued. "Did you see the young woman in white come in? Or go and sit on the bench?"

"No."

"As far as you know, did anyone from the cathedral staff see her come in or sit down? Perhaps there was someone with her?"

"I don't know."

Gombrowicz took over. "The duty guard also said he noticed her. He didn't see her come in or sit down, either, alone or with anyone else."

"And do you think she'd been sitting there long?"

The sacristan looked embarrassed. "I guess she'd been there a little while."

"Could you be more specific?"

"Since early morning. A little after we opened up, I'd say."

"And what time does the cathedral open?"

"At eight."

"Excuse me?"

"The cathedral opens at eight all year round. Why?"

"You're telling me this poor girl sat on this bench with her eyes wide open, in the middle of tourists and staff, and nobody noticed she was dead?"

"It's quite possible."

"It's quite possible? What do you mean, it's quite possible?"

"You know, mademoiselle, on average we have over fifty thousand visitors here every day. We can't put a guard on every tourist."

"Obviously not. Too busy chasing after bikinis. And yet you should have noticed this one, she was in a miniskirt."

Once again, the sacristan made eye contact with the police captain. Claire Kauffmann sent Gérard back to his sacristy and asked him to remain at the disposal of the authorities. Then she turned to the two police officers. "What about the tourist? The American? Where is she? Can we talk to her?"

Landard was finishing his cigarette with a slightly vacant expression. Gombrowicz, who was following the outline of a black paving stone with the tip of his foot, finally answered. "She's gone."

"Gone? What do you mean, gone?"

"The cathedral evacuated the tourists and the congregation right after the firefighters arrived. It seems the American got thrown out with the bathwater."

The magistrate raised her voice. "The cathedral? For heaven's sake. Just who is the cathedral?"

"I am the cathedral."

It was the taller and older of the two priests standing a few yards away who had spoken. The old man with the bald head went up to Claire Kauffmann stiffly, dressed in an elegant black suit where the only white that showed was the Roman Catholic clerical collar. He approached the young deputy magistrate, over whom he towered by a good eleven inches, and leaned a gaunt face toward her, cheeks covered with a carefully trimmed silvery beard. "I am Monsignor de Bracy, Rector of Notre Dame Cathedral in Paris. Whom do I have the honor of addressing, mademoiselle?"

She stated her name and job title. The prelate seemed surprised to be dealing with such a young-looking magistrate.

"I've already told these gentlemen from the police, to whom we are very grateful, mademoiselle, that I would appreciate it if you could keep me informed of the development of the investigation in real time, so to speak. Our archbishop, the cardinal, is currently away in the Philippines. I contacted him this morning and told him about this regrettable accident."

"We're talking about a murder, not an accident, monsieur."

"Monsignor."

"As for the investigation, Monsignor, you've already stuck your oar in by evacuating hundreds of potential witnesses before the investigators had even arrived."

The prelate scowled. "Mademoiselle, on average, fifty thousand visitors come to Notre Dame every day. Having been told that there was a deceased person within the cathedral walls, I thought it right not to offer her as a spectacle to a horde of Far Eastern tourists armed with camcorders and cameras. This is a place of prayer and contemplation, mademoiselle. Of course, it is also a tourist monument, and we sometimes regret this fact, trust me. However, what it certainly is not, and never will be, is the scene of a macabre spectacle to then be displayed all over the Internet. My dear young woman, I'd like to impress upon you that the place where you find yourself isn't just a piece of wasteland where the body of a drug addict or prostitute has been discovered. Do we understand each other?"

Her eyes raised to the prelate, Claire Kauffmann struggled to respond. Seeing he had reached his objective, the old man seemed to soften a little.

"Please be so kind as to let me know the name of the committing magistrate as soon as he's appointed."

He turned to Landard and Gombrowicz, and gave them a firm but warm handshake. "Goodbye, messieurs. I'm counting on you to allow us to reopen the cathedral very soon and, as much as possible, to keep reporters away. The cathedral suffers enough attacks as it is, without needing to be fed once again to the section of the press that's hostile to us. Of course, I remain at your full disposal for all that concerns the investigation, and will do my utmost to make your job as easy as possible. Good luck, captain. You will be kind enough to refrain from smoking inside the cathedral."

Father de Bracy walked away as he had come, with large strides, stiff and dignified, followed by Father Kern, who had been waiting for him at the entrance to the sacristy. Landard took the cigarette butt out of his mouth and drowned it in the nearest basin of holy water. Gombrowicz went over to him, smiling.

"Did you see how he cut the little deputy down to size?"

Landard took out his pack of cigarettes and immediately lit another one. "What do you make of the old man?"

"He's a bit like that actor, the tall one, you know, the one in Westerns."

"John Wayne?"

"That's it, John Wayne."

"I guess so. John Wayne in a cassock. With a beard and no hair."

"My cousin has a fifteen-year-old Great Dane that's his spitting image."

"Your cousin? The one who tinkers with cars near Porte de Bagnolet?"

"That's right."

"Do you ever go to Mass, Gombrowicz?"

"Me? No. Why?"

The medical examiner had just reappeared. Looking perplexed, he went to the magistrate and gestured at the two police officers to approach. "It happened roughly between ten p.m. and mid-night. It's possible she may have been moved after she died: the body is still quite rigid."

"Could she have been killed somewhere else, then brought here?"

"I'm not sure yet whether she was killed here or someplace else. I hope to be able to tell you more after the postmortem, madame."

"In any case, could she have spent the night on this bench?"

"It's the most likely theory."

The magistrate turned to Gombrowicz. "Is there a janitor here?"

The young lieutenant consulted his notes before replying. "He lives on the ground floor of the presbytery. Didn't see or hear anything. Slept like a log."

"Doesn't he do the rounds inside? I mean during the night?"

"Never."

"How do you know? Did you ask?"

"Of course, madame."

"And?"

"What for? At night the cathedral is locked. That's what he said, madame."

"I see. And when they opened it this morning, nobody noticed anything? The guard on duty, the sacristan, the priests, not to mention the hundreds of tourists who walked by for two hours and didn't notice she was dead?"

"Hundreds. I'd say thousands. I wrote down somewhere that in this cathedral on average ... Just a moment."

"Yes, I know, lieutenant, fifty thousand visitors every day. All right. Captain Landard, start the criminal investigation. Let's circulate the victim's photo in the press. Keep me posted when you discover anything about her identity. Doctor, will you make sure the body is removed? I must go, messieurs, I'm due at the Palais in less than five minutes."

The medical examiner had taken his glove off once again, and was scratching his head.

"Is there something else, doctor?"

"Yes, madame. Earlier, when I took her temperature, I noticed a detail. Actually, it's more than just a detail."

"Don't tell me she's been sexually abused. Here? In the middle of the cathedral?"

"One could say it's the opposite."

"What do you mean?"

"You see, madame, the entrance to the vagina is covered in wax."

"Say that again, doctor."

"After she died, her vagina was sealed with melted wax. To be precise, with candle wax."

Landard was hungry. Landard was bored. Crime scenes pissed him off to no end, with their packs of technicians and photographers in their immaculate overalls. You had to refrain from smoking, refrain from walking, refrain from coughing, and practically refrain from breathing. In his twenty years in the Crime Squad, he'd had time to watch and learn. In the easy cases, yes, the white suits proved useful. Sometimes, the work of the investigators was limited to waiting for the results of crime scene tests and post-mortems. A hair, a print, a trace of DNA, and problem solved. The judge would have his evidence, the judge would be delighted. So would the families of the victims, to whom science would give the irrefutable proof that allowed them to mourn in front of television cameras once the culprit was locked up. The investigators, the real ones, the ones who worked up a sweat in the field, could go home without even firing a shot, so to speak. The profession was becoming endangered.

During the course of the morning, three other Crime Squad officers from the same mold as Gombrowicz had been sent as support staff from the offices on Quai des Orfèvres. Less than five minutes' walk. A veritable neighborhood investigation. They had to question all the cathedral staff and anyone involved with the place, before letting them go for the rest of the day. Sacristans, guards, the man who kept all the keys, cleaning women, service technicians, the church's printer, postcard and rosary sellers, people who rented out audio guides, volunteer lecturers, organists, singers from the School of Music, clerks and, obviously, priests.

After the deputy had left, Landard delegated the management of all the interviews to Gombrowicz, and went back to look at the corpse. Still lying on the tiled floor, the poor girl was being photographed from every angle. If she'd known, would she have worn such a short dress the day before?

The medical examiner assured him that the body would be removed as soon as possible. The investigation, the real one, would begin late afternoon, after the white overalls had left, and after Gombrowicz had done the preliminary triage. Landard looked at his watch: ten to twelve. He had at least two hours for lunch.

Once he was out, he turned left, leaving behind the enormous line of visitors that had formed in front of the gates, still shut, of the cathedral, and which was now snaking around the whole width of the square. Monday, August 16th. The tourist season was in full swing. They could wait if they wanted, but the monument would reopen the following day at the earliest. For the time being, the cathedral had swapped its fifty thousand daily visitors, its priests, its masses, and its organ recitals, for a team of cops from the Quai.

He crossed Pont Marie, walked into the first brasserie, and sat indoors despite the heat, at a table with a stunning view of Notre Dame. He ordered steak tartare and fries, with a beer, then sank in his armchair, his hands crossed over his round stomach.

Landard was thinking.

First of all, coming across a deputy magistrate who was slightly interfering and full of initiative could be a good thing. This morning, for instance, it had allowed him, hands in his pockets and cigarette in his mouth, to calmly ogle little Kauffmann's thighs while she crouched by the corpse.

Landard ordered another beer.

Moreover, there were worse ways for a veteran of the Crime Squad to start the day than coming across a corpse like the pretty little thing still lying on the Notre Dame stone floor. Throughout his career, he'd seen all sorts of atrocities at all hours of day and night. He'd seen human flesh in quite a few forms: putrefied, burned, cut up, drowned, bled to death, riddled with bullets, busted with a baseball bat or an crowbar, dissolved in acid, slashed with a razor, eaten by dogs or rats, pulverized by the wheels of an underground or suburban train.

The waiter brought the steak tartare and Landard used the opportunity to order a third beer.

There was something exciting, sexually, of course, but also morally, about the dead woman in Notre Dame, with her clean little dress and her thighs exposed: a nauseating yet irrepressible feeling he had shared with all the men who'd seen or photographed her throughout the morning, including the priests—of that he was certain. There was something about this girl who was so pretty, so charming in that quiet death which made her look like a young woman asleep, that stimulated you, as though her death had to trigger in any good, self-respecting cop the desire to turn into a righter of wrongs and cut the balls off the bastard who'd dared kill such a beauty.

The waiter removed the carefully polished-off plate. Landard skipped the dessert list, and ordered coffee and a Calvados.

Finally, there was something eminently pleasing, from an intellectual point of view, about coming across a murderer who was clearly a fanatic but nevertheless discreet, intelligent, and well-organized. Because he must have wanted it at all costs, this staging of a death worthy of an occult thriller: a victim dressed in white, breathtakingly beautiful, found in the sanctuary of the Blessed Virgin, nobody with any idea of how she was placed there, a wax hymen reconstituted between her thighs.

A moralizer. Landard was dealing with a moralizer. A killer who wanted to restore the virginity of all the Paris girls in short outfits, and who'd staged this little number in order to make his mark. Landard was now certain—the murderer would revisit the scene of the crime. He wouldn't be able to stop himself, he'd be too eager to see the impact of his first sermon on people's minds.

At about a quarter past two, pleased with his work session, Landard asked for the bill and went downstairs to take a leak.

The cathedral looked like a huge police station, with plainclothes, uniformed, and overalled cops milling around. Leaving the technicians to work in the ambulatory, Gombrowicz and his three investigators had taken over the nave and divided it into four sections, which they'd turned into as many interrogation bureaus, so to speak. At the back of the church, spread over the rows of chairs usually reserved for worshippers, waited the entire Notre Dame staff. One by one, each employee, each priest, and each volunteer was called by a police officer to be questioned about that morning's events, or about a totally different incident possibly connected with the murder of the mysterious girl in white. Seen from a distance, with their buttocks on the edges of the thatched seats, their voices drowned in a murmur, their busts leaning forward toward men who appeared to be listening to them religiously, they could have been mistaken for sinners at the confessional, except it wasn't in a priest that they were confiding but in a police officer.

On his return, Landard found Lieutenant Gombrowicz in such a state of pronounced excitement that he wondered if his young subordinate had been drinking.

"I think we're making progress. Enormous progress. Apparently, it all happened yesterday afternoon. We have corroborating accounts."

Landard lit his umpteenth Gitane and blew the smoke toward the high vaults of the nave. The curls rolled over themselves before dissipating in the incense-steeped air. "Go on, Gombrowicz. I'm all ears."

The day before, the ceremony of the Assumption had been disrupted by an incident, right in the midst of the Marian procession, as an unbroken line of ten thousand worshippers was stretching out under the blazing sun between Île Saint-Louis and Île de la Cité, and loudspeakers fitted on four vans were blasting Hail Marys at full volume. There had been an altercation, brief but violent, between a cathedral regular and an unknown woman dressed in white. At the head of the procession, just a few yards from the silver statue of the Virgin carried by six knights of the Holy Sepulcher, before the incredulous eyes of auxiliary bishop Monsignor Rieux Le Molay, the priests of Notre Dame, and numerous witnesses, a young-looking man with blond, curly hair had tried to exclude the young woman from the procession, pushing her onto the sidewalk, waving a crucifix, and finally using it as a weapon to try to hit her in the face. One of the cathedral guards, Mourad, had intervened to separate them, helped the victim up, and sent the aggressor unceremoniously to the back of the procession.

Landard put out his cigarette in the nearest holy water basin and cleared his throat. It was his cue to step onto the stage. "Your auxiliary bishop, yesterday ..."

"Rieux Le Molay?"

"Can we see him?"

"He's gone."

"Where?"

"To Lourdes."

"Since when?"

"This morning. He took an early train."

"So the cardinal's gone to the folks with slanting eyes, and the bishop's in Lourdes. Great. All the bosses here are packing their bags."

"No wonder. They've left the shop and the hassle to the old rector."

"What about this Mourad? Has he also retreated to his mud hut?"

Gesturing at the first row of employees, Gombrowicz summoned a man built like a tank, wearing a tired blazer, woolen trousers that were too thick for that time of year, and a carabiner on his belt from which jangled at least twenty keys.

"Are you Mourad?"

"Yes, monsieur."

"Were you here this morning?"

"No, monsieur, I started work at twelve-thirty because I finished late last night."

"And what did they tell you when you arrived today?"

"I was surprised the cathedral was shut. I thought, 'There's been a problem, Mourad.' I called my morning colleague. He was still inside even though normally he'd have been on his lunch break. It was he, and a policeman, who let me in."

"Did they tell you what happened?"

"They said they'd found a girl at the back of the cathedral."

"So, tell me, Mourad, you were working yesterday?"

"Yes, monsieur. Twelve-thirty to ten-thirty p.m."

"And how did it go?"

"Yesterday?"

"Yesterday. Try and tell me in detail."

"August fifteenth, like Christmas, is one of the most difficult days of the year. At twelve-forty-five, there's the Assumption mass, at three-forty-five the Assumption vespers, at ten past four the Assumption procession starts, they take out the large silver statue of the Virgin and everyone has to follow. Priests, faithful, tourists—everybody. Nobody is allowed to stay behind in the cathedral. We always have to negotiate with the little old ladies who want to wait inside but we follow the rector's instructions: there mustn't be anybody in the cathedral until the procession returns at about six. Once everyone's out, the other guards and I shut the gates and we join the procession."

"Whereabouts were you in the procession?"

"At the head. They always put me at the head, with the bishop, the priests, and the statue of the Virgin."

"Why you?"

"Because I'm the strongest among the guards. Usually, if there's any problem, it's at the head of the procession."

"And what kind of problem could there be, Mourad?"

"How should I know? Somebody could attack the bishop or the statue of the Virgin."

"You think so? Who'd do such a thing?"

"How should I know? The people from Act Up, for instance."

"Act Up? What—the queers?"

"I'm just saying for example. About ten days ago, they staged a sort of a raid inside the cathedral, to protest against what the Pope says about condoms. They put up banners, tried to chain themselves to the entrance gates. They were quite forceful. There were journalists, cameras, TV people."

"Quite a goddam mess then."

"Oh, yeah!"

"As a matter of fact, Mourad, yesterday afternoon, during the procession, didn't you have a little problem?"

"Yes, a fight. There's one or two every year. Usually, it's old ladies fighting to get into the cathedral first after the procession."

"Very pious, these old women—are they?"

"It's the fact that, once inside, they want a seat."

"But the fight yesterday, it wasn't between old women, was it?"

"No, they were young people."

"So tell me exactly what happened, Mourad."

"There was this guy—we know him well—he's been coming here for months. He's a bit—how can I put it?"

"A bit of an oddball."

"That's right, a bid of an oddball. Sometimes, it's as if he thinks the Virgin Mary's his sister, you know? Or his mother."

"I get the picture, yes."

"He prays and cries at her feet. Lies down on the stone floor, takes pictures of her, tries to touch her, brings her flowers. Every evening, when we close up, it's always the same thing. He doesn't want to leave, he wants to stay and sleep with the Virgin of the Pillar."

"Which one's the Virgin of the Pillar?"

"It's the statue over there, to the right of the podium. She's the one on all the postcards, guidebooks, candles."

"On the candles, too?"

"Yes, sure, on the candles, look."

Mourad went to get a candle from one of the stands.

"And so this guy who's so in love with the Virgin Mary, who did he try to beat up?"

"This girl in white walking next to it."

"Next to what?"

"Next to the statue of the Virgin. She'd been walking there since the start of the procession. Next to it, in front of it. It's true that after a while, she was beginning to disturb everyone."

"Who's everyone?"

"The auxiliary bishop, the priests, the knights. Everybody, really."

"Who are these knights, again?"

"The Knights of the Holy Sepulcher, the ones who carry the silver statue of the Virgin on its stretcher. It must weigh at least four hundred and fifty pounds, you know."

"And why would this girl have disturbed your knights?"

"Because she was very beautiful and her dress was very short. At one point, the Head Honcho even asked me to go talk to her."

"Who's the Head Honcho?"

"The rector. It's what we call him among ourselves, but don't go repeating it."

"So the Head Honcho himself told you to go to the chick in the miniskirt, to ask her to walk farther away, otherwise the knights, the priests, and the auxiliary bishop would be sweating buckets. Is that right?"

Mourad just smiled in reply.

"And so what did the girl say to you?"

"I didn't get a chance to speak to her because the other guy went for her. Grabbed her by the hair, started shaking her, calling her a prostitute, a whore, a slut, all sorts of stuff. That she should leave the Virgin Mary alone, that she should follow her example, that the Virgin is the woman above all women."

"And what did you do at that point, Mourad?"

"I grabbed the kid by the neck and flattened him on the ground with my knee. Then I asked the girl if she was OK, if she wanted me to call the police, because her lip was bleeding a bit."

"And?"

"Well, she didn't want to call the police. She said, 'What are you doing here? Why are you working for these people?'"

"What did she mean by that?"

"How should I know?"

Gombrowicz had been fidgeting for a while, ever since Mourad had started talking about the attack. "Tell him, Mourad, tell him what you told me earlier. What language was the girl speaking?"

"With me? Well, Arabic, of course."

Landard burst out laughing. "You're right, Mourad, what else could you and she have been speaking? After all, we're in France, right? And then?"

"Then I told the kid I didn't want to see him for the rest of the day. He ran away saying it was a topsy-turvy world, and telling me to go back home."

"And what do you think he meant by that, Mourad?"

Mourad looked intently into Landard's eyes. "You know perfectly well what he meant, inspector."

Landard rummaged in his jacket pocket but could find only a dark blue, crushed, empty pack. "OK, Mourad. And then what happened?"

"Then the procession went back into the cathedral for Solemn Mass."

"And was the girl in white at Solemn Mass?"

"In the front row, with her legs crossed."

"All right. And then?"

"Then, at the end of the Mass, at about eight p.m., we emptied the cathedral, so we could put up the tulle."

"The tulle?"

"On summer evenings, we stretch a huge canvas across the transept, because at nine-thirty p.m., we reopen the cathedral for *Rejoice, Mary*."

"What's *Rejoice, Mary*?"

"It's a film about the Assumption."

"Of course, stupid question. So at half past nine, you reopened the doors once again and people came back in, like a movie theater."

"That's right."

"And at what time did *Rejoice, Mary* finish?"

"The film is forty-five minutes long. At ten-thirty p.m., we got everyone out again."

"And was the girl in white also there for *Rejoice, Mary*?"

"I couldn't tell you."

"You didn't see her?"

"No."

"After Mass you didn't see her again for the rest of the evening?"

"No."

"And were there many people at *Rejoice, Mary* last night?"

"It was full. Over a thousand people."

"What do you do inside? Is it like a movie theater? Do you dim the lights?"

"We just keep the night-lights on in the entrance. The night-lights and the candles."

"And can people come and go as they please?"

"As they please, yes."

"And you never have any problems?"

"What kind of problems?"

"I don't know, couples smooching in the corners, kids trying to remain locked in the cathedral overnight so they can piss in the holy water basins."

"Very seldom. In any case, after we close, we do the rounds to check everything properly."

"Hard work, all that, Mourad."

"I told you. Along with Christmas, it's the hardest day of the year."

"Because of the crowds?"

"The crowds, the crazy people."

"And tell me, Mourad, where do you live?"

" In Garges-lès-Gonesse. Why?"

"It's quite a trek home."

"I take the local train D, from Châtelet. Then the bus. Then there's a bit on foot."

"Are there still buses in Gonesse when you lock up here?"

"I generally miss the last one."

"So what do you do?"

"I walk."

"You walk all the way from the train station?"

"I have to."

"You don't have a car?"

"Can't afford one."

"If you leave here at about ten-thirty—eleven, what time do you get home?"

Mourad did not answer.

"Are you sure you did your rounds last night, Mourad?"

"What are you trying to say, inspector?"

"Don't get excited, Mourad, I'm just asking you a question. After such a long day you must have just wanted to go home to bed, right? I'm trying to put myself in your shoes. If I'd had the chance to catch my train fifteen minutes earlier by skipping my rounds, I wouldn't have hesitated, trust me. Hell, the last bus in Gonesse, that's vital."

"Last night I did my rounds like I do them every time I get to lock up in the evening, inspector. Do you have any other questions or may I leave?"

"You can go home."

"The girl they found this morning, is it her? Is it the girl in white who got attacked yesterday?"

"You've got it exactly right, Mourad. You should join the police."

The guard walked away, and his keychain kept jingling in time with his footsteps long after Landard lost sight of him behind a pillar.

"Gombrowicz, have you got a cigarette?"

Gombrowicz took a pack of Camel Lights out of his jeans pocket and offered it to Landard. The latter pulled out a cigarette, made a face, put it between his lips, then shook his lighter for a long time without managing to light it.

"Do you have a light, Gombrowicz?"

"No. Just use a candle."

Landard went up to a rack, grabbed a lit candle with a picture of the Virgin of the Pillar, and took a long drag on his cigarette. He remained lost in his thoughts in the midst of a thickening cloud of smoke. Then he suddenly waved the air away as though to clear his head, and turned to Gombrowicz.

"Hey, Gombrowicz. What do you bet Mourad didn't do his rounds last night?"

⚜

Father Kern was going home, his head buzzing and his body weary. In the square, amid idle tourists, Eiffel Tower trinket sellers, and gypsy beggars, the woman whom guards and sacristans nicknamed Madame Pipi seemed to be dozing on a bench in the shade of Charlemagne's equestrian statue. A little earlier that morning, she had been syphoned out as part of the general evacuation ordered by the cathedral rector. His thoughts still absorbed by the image of the dead young woman lying on the stone floor, Kern with his eyes had absentmindedly followed the eccentric old lady's absurd, flowery hat. He'd seen it struggling to stay afloat above the noisy flood of tourists pushed toward the emergency exit, tossed about like a wisp of straw, desperately trying to swim against the current, losing a few plastic poppies on the way, and finally vanishing into the whirlwind funnel of the Portal of the Last Judgment.

When the priest walked past her, she seemed to miraculously wake up from her nap. She gave him a worried look, bordering on panic, as usual, and made an unsure gesture at him. Kern reciprocated her greeting and picked up the pace. Not today. Not now. This time she'd have to wait to tell him about her apocalyptic visions, her paranoid delirium, and the satanic attacks only she had been chosen to witness, as well as the dazzling retaliations to which only the Virgin seemed to hold the secret. Kern didn't know what kind of chaotic path could have led Madame Pipi to that permanent chair in Notre Dame, three or four yards from the Virgin of the Pillar where, every morning, she came to lay her anguish. What could she have possibly suffered that she now came to seek, like a daily fix, the benevolent gaze of the marble Madonna? Nobody among the cathedral staff knew anything, or at least not much, about the old lady with the flowery hat. They didn't even know her name. Very few priests had heard her confession. All that could be gathered about her was that she'd had a youth marked by a violent father; fear was her constant traveling companion, followed by solitude, then a slow descent into a kind of mental confinement, an increasing dependence on things religious, and a more and more airtight mutism from which she always seemed about to emerge but never succeeded. In other words, she suffered from the kind of—hateful as the term may be—madness that some cathedral regulars sometimes appeared to border on.

Over the course of the eleven summers he spent neglecting his Poissy parish in order to stand in at Notre Dame during the month of August, Father Kern had had the time to get to know these cathedral strays. In that respect, it was probably not very different from the Middle Ages: the cathedral doors were open all day to those damaged by life, those who couldn't find their place in a brutal world reserved for the strong, a world they'd been hurled into by an accident of birth, and who, in their search for a bubble of comfort or illusion, had found refuge in this huge church at the heart of Île de la Cité. There were quite a few of them, men and women, who, every morning, as soon as the cathedral opened, would go into the nave, to a chair they'd abandoned the day before, and stay there until evening, impervious to the army of tourists invading the aisles. These strays seemed to float between two worlds, staring into space or at a Virgin, a figure of Christ, or a candle, for hours on end. Nobody would ever think of moving them. Sometimes, you had to gently hush them when they entered into direct communication with God or Mary, and engaged in an overly loud conversation. And every so often, you had to take a rag and wipe up the floor under their chairs.

This time, however, Father Kern was going home and his heart would be, like the cathedral doors, exceptionally shut for a few hours.

On the suburban train taking him back to Poissy, he tried to put some order in his thoughts. First, there was the haunting image of the girl lying on the stone floor, tragic and immodest, discovered just as he was starting the *Salve Regina* in the chancel.

Then there was the irruption of this army of police, pistols at their belts, into a sanctuary, that, since the dawn of time, people had been entering in peace, having left their weapons outside. But perhaps that was mere illusion. Perhaps evil and violence had wormed their way in through the impenetrable stones of the cathedral long ago. Perhaps the battle between light and darkness had been raging within the centuries-old walls forever. And perhaps it was more intensely violent there than outside.

A little earlier that afternoon, a young investigator from the Crime Squad had questioned him, along with all the other priests and the rest of the staff. He'd had to recall the events of the previous day. The holy masses, the crowds, the noise, the procession, and the stifling heat. The hymns, the prayers, and the Ave Maria through the sound system. The moments of silent contemplation. Again, the crowds and the heat. And that provocatively beautiful young woman, so visible, so radiant, so mesmerizing, deliberately served up to the eyes of the six Knights of the Holy Sepulcher at the head of the procession. Restricted in their three-piece suits, wearing white gloves, wrapped in their cavalry capes bearing the scarlet cross of Jerusalem. Sweating under a blazing sun, staggering under the weight of a stretcher carrying the silver statue of the Virgin. Their eyes bulging, bloodshot. Was it the physical strain? Or the pain from the weight of the statue digging into their shoulders? Or the sight of this girl parading right under their noses and the inebriating clicking of her heels on the asphalt? And what about the twenty or so priests marching behind the knights? Brief, furtive side glances from surplice-wearing colleagues, sliding from top to toe and from toe to top, to better caress with their eyes—in spite of themselves and the liturgical dress—the shape, the curve of the buttocks, the outline of the legs of this girl who was walking in very high-heeled pumps, parallel to the procession. And what about the auxiliary bishop, Monsignor Rieux Le Molay? Wedged between the knights and the troop of priests, his miter and crozier towering over the crowd, his hand stroking the air in an infinite repetition of signs of the cross, again, and again, and again. And sometimes, as his fingers would complete the gesture on the right hand side—not always, but sometimes—his eyes would veer slightly, a little beyond the imaginary cross that was already evaporating in the heat, and his gaze would caress, even just for a second, even in the midst of a circular glance, the beautiful white form, the slender ankles, the bend of the calves, the tanned thighs that disappeared under an unreasonably short skirt. The temptation of lust. A man who asks to emerge for an imperceptible instant from the heavy cope embroidered with gold thread.

After all, hadn't the entire Île de la Cité ogled her with desire? Hadn't the whole of Paris? And in the end, like a thunderstorm tearing through an overcharged sky, there had been this absurd fight with the blond young worshipper, who looked quietly insane and harmless, but who had suddenly given in to violence. What had happened? And who was that girl? They'd found her the following morning, dead. What was the real truth?

Naturally, the police had questioned him about the incident at the Assumption. Who was the blond boy with the pale, angelic face? Did he know his name? Had he been coming to the cathedral for long? Had he ever shown any signs of violence? Had he heard his confession?

All Father Kern could do was shrug at these questions. Yes, he knew the young man, but only by sight. No, he didn't know his name. He'd never heard his confession. And even if he had, a priest wasn't expected to ask to see the ID of a sinner come to ask the Lord's forgiveness. No, as far as he knew, the boy had never been violent. He was one of them. One of the Notre Dame strays whose immovable figure appeared every morning amid the rows of chairs.

One day—as it happens, during confession—a young woman with a slightly unhinged expression, an eight a.m. Mass regular, had opened her purse and revealed a half-rusted bread knife. "In case I get attacked by the devil," she'd said. Father Kern had not thought it appropriate to point her out to the duty guard, since he judged a satanic attack to be highly unlikely. Had he been wrong not to? Were the Notre Dame strays crazy to the point of being dangerous?

These thoughts kept going around and around in his head until he reached his presbytery. The bell of his parish was ringing six p.m. He'd barely shut the door behind him when the phone rang.

"François? It's Monsignor de Bracy."

"Yes, Monsignor."

"You got home alright?"

"Yes, Monsignor."

"Have you also been questioned by the police?"

"Yes, Monsignor."

"What did they ask you?"

"They're interested in yesterday's incident during the procession."

"Naturally. They're making a connection with this morning's grisly discovery. That's really bad publicity. And that unfortunate girl. Did you know her, François? Had you seen her in the cathedral before?"

"No, Monsignor, never. I mean not until the ceremony on August fifteenth."

"Neither had I. To be honest, I'm not really sure what she was doing there, in that inappropriate attire."

"Any news about when we'll reopen?"

"I've just spoken to Captain Landard. He wishes to reopen from tomorrow. That's good, even though we'll probably have a crowd of journalists on our backs first thing."

"Isn't it a bit soon, Monsignor? Wouldn't it be better to wait for the first conclusions of the inquest or the appointment of an investigating magistrate?"

"I understand where you're coming from, François. However, I'm obliged to make a decision now. Considering the time difference with Manila, I won't be able to reach the cardinal archbishop before midnight tonight. As for Monsignor Rieux de Molay, ever since he left for Lourdes early this morning, all I'm getting is his voice mail."

"I see. So you're hoping to reopen soon?"

"From my point of view, the sooner the better. The Virgin Mary's faithful are claiming their home back. Besides, I get the impression the police want to check the old adage that a murderer always revisits the scene of his crime."

"If the young man is guilty of anything, do you really think he'll come back to loiter in the vicinity?"

"I don't know, François. I don't possess your in-depth knowledge of criminals. In any event, I simply wanted to let you know about the cathedral reopening and that I'll see you tomorrow morning. Have a good evening, François."

"You, too, Monsignor."

At the very moment he was putting down the receiver, he noticed red marks on his wrists. He calmly removed his jacket, on the lapel of which a small Roman cross was pinned, and inspected his forearms. The marks went all the way up above his elbows. He knew what they meant. The disease was upon him again. Over the days that followed, he would be the scene of a struggle, another battle to fight, to add to the countless list of crises that had attacked him since his early childhood. The treatment for them had abruptly stunted his growth and made him into that four-foot-ten, ninety-five-pound ectoplasm in priest's clothes.

TUESDAY

KNEELING IN FRONT OF THE LARGE, CRUCIFIED CHRIST NAILED to the south wall, hands joined under his chin and lips moving silently, Gombrowicz was praying. Except that what he was hearing was in no way the voice of God. The voice speaking to him through the earpiece belonged to his superior in the Crime Squad, Captain Landard.

"Don't overdo it, Gombrowicz. You look like a little girl in white ankle socks, taking her First Communion."

Gombrowicz raised his hands a couple of inches and whispered into the microphone he'd pinned to the cuff of his shirtsleeve. "My knees are beginning to ache. How do they manage to stay like this for so long without moving? There's an old woman next to me and she's been praying non-stop for half an hour. Still as a statue."

Landard burst out laughing. "Perhaps she's dead, too. Give her a little nudge and see if she comes crashing down on the stone floor."

"No chance. I can guarantee this one's virginity is still intact. No need to recork it with wax."

Shortly before opening time, Landard had set up his plan

of action. Besides Gombrowicz, whom he'd positioned next to
the Portal of Saint Anne, and who was keeping an eye on the
entrance, three young athletic-looking lieutenants, with fanny
packs containing their service weapons across their chests, had
been deployed in the nave, camouflaged as worshippers or low
budget tourists. At regular intervals, a pickpocket caught red-
handed would bear the brunt of this, to say the least, unusual
concentration of police forces in this place that represented a
strong temptation for the petty thieves of Paris.

Landard was settled at the helm of the cathedral audio-visual
control room situated above the sacristy. Sitting at the console
littered with blinking diodes, his walkie-talkie within easy reach,
the captain acted like a minor monarch surveying his kingdom
through cameras arranged all around the nave, which were generally used to film the great Sunday Mass for the Catholic TV
channel, KTO. Mourad, whom Landard had practically requi-
sitioned to guide him through the mosaic of plans and views
of Notre Dame before him, was at his side. When the moment
came, Mourad would be able—at least so Landard hoped—to
point out, on one of the control room screens, the suspect's
blond head amid the crowd of anonymous tourists.

The police had been waiting since morning, and the entire
cathedral seemed to be holding its breath, gurgling with rumors,
while waiting for the one all the Notre Dame staff was now calling "the blond angel." A priest had come to say the two morning
masses, interpreting with odd falseness a role he had nevertheless been playing for years. The duty sacristan, the guards, the
reception staff, the volunteer speakers, the morning faithful,
even tourists from the other end of the world, all seemed to be
acting like automatons, as though absent, their eyes on that fixed
point Gombrowicz was also staring at: the Portal of Sainte Anne,
through which, sooner or later, the main suspect of a sordid mur-

der case would, according to police sources, walk in and thrust himself into the net cast by the Crime Squad. Meanwhile, outside, on the square, a team from the TV station France 3 Île-de-France was installing a camera in anticipation of the lunchtime news, and they were soon joined by a van from the LCI station.

"Landard to Gombrowicz. Landard to Gombrowicz."

"I'm listening, Landard."

"Still nothing?"

"There are some Japanese, Germans, more Japanese."

"What the fuck is he doing? Keep your eyes open, guys. The kid isn't far, I can feel it."

Sitting in one of the chapels south of the principal nave, just a few yards away from the crucified Christ beneath which Gombrowicz was revising his catechism, Father Kern was waiting. He was waiting for those worshippers, French or foreign, who wanted to see a priest. In the chapel dedicated to confession, a few years earlier, they had installed a large glass cage aimed at ensuring calm and confidentiality to both the one hearing confession and the one making confession. Ever since, the cathedral priests had called this chapel "the jar."

Sitting at the bottom of his jar, Father Kern was waiting: like almost everybody else this morning, he was waiting for a young man with blond, curly hair and a vaguely romantic, slender look, who, two days earlier, had attacked a young woman with a crucifix. The young woman had been found dead, and the blond angel seemed to be up to his neck in trouble.

Sitting at his small confession table on which he usually kept two dictionaries—English and Spanish—Father Kern was waiting: waiting for night to inevitably fall over the city. In about ten hours at most, the red marks would reappear on his arms, ankles, and calves, just as the evening before, but this time they'd be accompanied by a violent bout of fever. The sharp, unbearable joint pain would probably come tomorrow. He knew this from past experience. The disease had definitely returned, attacking his body night after night, growing more intense day by day. How long would the crisis last? A week? A month? A year? Father Kern really couldn't tell.

Claire Kauffmann had barely slept a wink all night. She had watched the hours go by on the fluorescent screen of her alarm clock, tossing and turning in her sheets as she sighed, so much so that Peanuts, her cat, who snuggled up to her every night, this time had decided to abandon the quilted softness of the comforter in favor of the calmer kitchen floor. Usually, she managed to leave outside her bedroom door the images collected during her office hours at the Palais de Justice. She'd seen the worst one could possibly see. Besides, her bedroom had been furnished, decorated, and designed to give her, at least during the night, a few hours of amnesia, and to constitute an effective citadel against the violence of the city. The metal blinds were always down. The heavy velvet curtains always closed. The door was padded. The carpet was deep. On the wall and on the shelves, there were childhood mementoes, a couple of plush toys, a pair of white shoes with straps worn only for one evening before she'd tipped into adolescence. Objects she liked to feel surrounded by when, alone in the dark, she felt sucked in by her thoughts, fears, and memories.

However, that night, Claire Kauffmann wasn't able to throw the black veil of sleep over the image of the white Madonna found strangled on the stone floor in Notre Dame. Just as she would start to doze off, no sooner was her body about to abandon itself than the cathedral images would come back to mind.

Not images from her working morning, not those of the investigation in progress, not those of a place filled with the reassuring presence of uniforms and technicians in white smocks, and illumined by powerful projectors that lit even the darkest corners. What Claire Kauffmann saw as soon as she closed her eyes, curled up deep in her bed, was the endless night before; it was the screams of the young woman in white echoing in the blackness of the huge church, that brought no response, no help, as she faced her murderer alone. It was as though an iron hand was forcing her, a magistrate of the French Republic, to watch the squalid spectacle of death going over a woman's body, spreading open her thighs, caressing an oddly hairless, adolescent sex, and finally bringing close a candle that had just poured an obscene light over her skin. Then, as an extra step deeper into the nightmare, Claire Kauffmann would quit her position as spectator. The hand that held her by the wrist so tightly she felt like screaming along with the victim, would then force her to approach the dark silhouette busying itself over the corpse dressed in white. And all of a sudden, the magistrate would realize that the victim's hair was not dark but blond, blond like her own, and she'd immediately feel the murderer's clumsy touch on her own skin, the candle scorching her own thighs. She would try to scream but no sound would come out of her mouth. She would struggle but her body, as though dead, no longer belonged to her. Finally, she would open her eyes, breathless, her sheets drenched in sweat, and put the light back on, trying to fill her lungs with air, trying to slow down her breathing, trying to fix her eyes on a familiar object on her bedroom walls.

Women constantly had to pay when confronted with men's urges, whether sexual or murderous. Even in death, that girl had had to suffer the insults of a pervert. With candle wax. And what else? That's not counting the invasive, suggestive looks of

all those—police officers, technicians, onlookers, and tourists—
who had paraded around her body. And yet the ordeal wasn't
quite over yet. There was still the postmortem, which would
deflower her a little further. She kept picturing the medical
examiner, a highly professional man with whom she'd worked
several times in the past, scratching his scalp after removing his
latex glove. She would then turn around in bed for the umpteenth time, and curl up even more.

When the alarm went off, Claire Kauffmann got out of bed,
still groggy from her nocturnal struggle between wakefulness
and nightmare. She fed Peanuts. She drank her hot chocolate
while listening to the radio news. At the end of the seven a.m.
headlines, France Info had mentioned the Notre Dame murder.
The press knew, so the whole media circus would now begin.

Then Claire Kauffmann had a shower, displaying her nudity
only to the eyes of Peanuts, who was lying in a corner, lazily
slapping his tail on the bathroom floor. She got dressed, shielded
her body, still damp, with a cotton bodysuit, carefully fastening
the crotch, covered her legs and buttocks with a sheer summer
pantyhose, sheathing, as she did every morning, her blond sex
with at least two protective layers.

She took the bus from the 17th arrondissement, where
she lived, deploring the promiscuity, the forced contact, men's
sometimes insistent looks. Sometimes she'd be followed, over the
course of the journey, by slimy types whose eyes she felt ogling
her back. She wasn't sure which were worse: those who, wretched
and stammering, ended up slipping her their phone numbers, or
those who didn't come out with it but preferred to lag a few steps
behind her, hands in their pockets, eyes on her behind.

She arrived at the Palais half an hour late and her fellow deputy, with whom she shared an office, remarked on how unusual
that was. She got down to work, reading, filing, taking notes, a

Sisyphus with a pencil skirt and a blond bun, who tried every day without success to reduce the mountain of files on her desk. Finally, at about eleven-thirty, she made up her mind to call Captain Landard on his cell phone, seeing how he'd neglected to keep her informed of the progress of his investigation at Notre Dame.

She found him highly agitated. At the other end of the line, Landard was speaking in a whisper and Claire Kauffmann struggled to make out everything he was saying.

"I'm telling you, the kid's here, Mademoiselle Kauffmann, the blond angel, in the cathedral, he came back, I was right. I saw him arrive on my control screen like an apparition, less than ten minutes ago, he was all you could see, he was almost fluorescent. Mourad, the guard who collared him the day before yesterday, has formally identified him. And guess where the kid went right away? Go on, guess, madame. Guess what the little bastard did as soon as he came in?"

"How should I know, captain?"

"I'll tell you, madame. You'll never guess. The son of a bitch went to confession."

The blond angel had been confessing for half an hour. Unable to bear it any longer, Landard had left the control room to go see the scene with his own eyes. Shut up in his jar, as though put under glass like an extraordinary butterfly, the kid was talking endlessly, laughing, crying, shaking his head, gesticulating. And who was he confessing to? To a diminutive priest, almost a midget, who was listening without saying a word, resting his chin on his fist and who, every few minutes, would simply nod.

Landard was chomping at the bit. He felt like a ten-year-old with an empty stomach and saliva in the corners of his mouth, his nose glued to the window of a delicatessen shop. He'd given the rector his word that very morning: no scandal or arrests inside the cathedral. They'd have to wait for the blond angel to come back out before picking him up. Outside, everything was ready: two officers had been repositioned at the exit and a third at the entrance, in case the suspect decided to lose them from the rear, in addition to Gombrowicz, still beneath his large crucified Christ, less than ten paces from the confessional. In case of serious problems, there were always the uniformed police in the square, placed there with the rector's agreement, to keep the demands of the TV reporters at bay.

Landard reluctantly went to kneel next to his lieutenant, his eyes not turned up, but constantly flitting toward the suspect. "What do you think they're telling each other in there?"

"Perhaps we should have placed a mic."

"The priest wouldn't have agreed. What you say inside there is confidential, you know. Who could have guessed that the kid would be devious enough as to go and confess?"

"Don't worry, Landard. He'll get to confess again before the evening, and this time at the Quai."

Somewhat reassured by the prospect of the forthcoming interrogation, Landard went back to his prayers. Still, the blond angel didn't seem to want to come out and Landard, whose knees where beginning to ache, realized the absurdity of the situation.

Finally, he made a decision. After all, he had his man shut up in a hermetic cage. What was he waiting for? For the bird to fly away? To hell with the promise made to the rector. It was time to intervene. He stepped out of the suspect's sight and, with a whisper into his walkie-talkie, summoned the three lieutenants waiting outside. Then, as soon as the reinforcements had arrived, without any other procedure, Landard opened the glass door of the confessional and let his men loose inside, the way he would have let dogs loose in a butcher's shop.

The loud, metallic noise of the door bounced off the walls of the cell. There were posters of bare-breasted girls next to a postcard of a Van Gogh landscape, a group of crows flying over a field of wheat. The prisoner raised his shaved head to the visitor, got off his stool, and held out a hand on which a tattoo in the form of a snake began, then disappeared beneath the turned-up sleeve and seemed to go up the entire length of his arm.

"Is it Thursday already? I miscalculated the days, François. I'm really losing it. Hours, days, time in general."

Father Kern reassured the prisoner. "It's me who's come early, Djibril. It's Tuesday."

Djibril sat back down, yawned, rubbed his eyes with the back of his hand and, with a gesture, offered his bed as a seat to the visiting priest.

"Coffee?"

Kern nodded. Djibril took a jar of Nescafé from a shelf, poured an estimated amount of coffee into a glass, and put an electric kettle on.

"Black, as usual?"

"Yes, please, Djibril, black."

Kern sat on the bed. They waited without speaking for the kettle to boil. Djibril filled the glass, immersed the spoon in it, and the sound of metal hitting against the sides reminded him of the key turning in his cell door, in the evening. Then he handed the coffee to the priest.

"Mind your fingers, it's hot."

Father Kern stirred the coffee. He was watching the coffee dissolve in silence, felt the smell rise to his nostrils, and the heat turning his fingers red. Yet he didn't put the glass down, as though he wasn't there, as though he was insensitive to the burn.

"I thought you were at Notre Dame on Tuesdays."

Kern gave him a vague smile. "I'm going to give you a child's answer: school closed early today." He took a sip and held out his glass. "On second thought, I'll have a lump of sugar. I didn't have a chance to have lunch." Referring to the television set mounted on the wall, which was showing the muted images of a German police series, he said, "Did you see the one o'clock news?"

"I did, yes. Nothing else to do here. They brought your murderer out right through the main door, right under the noses of the cameras. And the prize for best direction goes to the Paris Police Headquarters for its spectacular cinematography."

"The journalists were well informed. I guess the cathedral people couldn't help talking. They already knew about the attack on Assumption Day. They knew who the police had set a trap for. And the kid swam right into the net thinking he was coming to confess. Did they show his face on television?"

"They put a jacket over his head. Then they stuffed him into a car and put a revolving light on the roof. What a bunch of clowns! I mean, Police Headquarters is five hundred yards away."

"He's just a boy, Djibril, he's lost. They came to get him while I was giving him absolution. It took four of them to push him down to the floor."

"You absolved a murderer? I guess you'll say that's what you always do when you're here. Every Thursday, you talk to and forgive guys who got life."

"Who said the boy's the killer?"

"Seems the press has already tried him. You think he's innocent?"

"I think he's terribly guilty. Guilty of having misinterpreted the Scriptures, of turning the Virgin into an idol, of having given in to easy intolerance, easy stupidity. This boy is crazy and lost. He's not a murderer. He didn't kill that girl."

"How can you be so sure?"

"I'm not sure of anything, Djibril. It's just that the boy came to me. He confided during confession. He told me about his obsessions, his confused sexuality, his Virgin Mary fetish, his urges. He told me about the attack the day before yesterday. I agree that he needs help. But he said that after the incident at the procession, he went home to bed."

"Did you tell the police that?"

"Naturally, they asked me to repeat the entire conversation to them."

"And?"

"Let's just say that I didn't tell them everything. I used the argument of the secrecy of confession."

Djibril put the kettle back on and opened the jar of Nescafé again.

"The crazy kid reminds you of your brother, doesn't he?"

Kern stared into his glass and, for a few seconds, toyed with the tip of his spoon. In the fifteen years he'd been visiting Poissy as prison chaplain, he'd met a lot of prisoners. Most of them had no interest in religion but needed an attentive ear in which to confide, someone outside the circle of the prison administration, who would sit and listen to them without judgment. After all, they'd already had their trial, their guilt had been established by a magistrate and reinforced by a prosecutor, and they were not about to forget that. The Law had sentenced most of them to fifteen years to life: only those with heavy sentences were locked up at Poissy.

There, he'd met Djibril. A six-foot-six giant weighing two

hundred and forty pounds, with a shaved head, and covered in tattoos. Sentenced to life imprisonment with a minimum of twenty-two years before parole. A holdup gone wrong; a gas station in Beauce, a female cashier taken as hostage, several hours of siege by Special Forces, a risky exit improvised on an impulse or rather panic, under the influence of alcohol found on the premises and consumed in order to silence fear; at the end of the night and the terror, there was a dead gendarme, the father of an eleven-year-old child, lying in his own blood at the foot of a pump of Lead-Free 98. And so, contrary to expectations, a bond had formed between the priest and the murderer. Over the months, Djibril had opened up. He'd told his story to the little man with a cross on his lapel. It had been quite a long fall, actually, which had started on the top floors of a high-rise in Montreuil. A lookout, then a petty dealer, then the head of a gang. Expulsion from school. Gradual alienation from the family and several stints in jail. The first contact with a different kind of boss, the kind who isn't interested in small-time but in jewelry stores, banks, and security transport. A difference in scale, from block to district, from district to town, from town to region, then to the entire country. Also, the first nicknames—the Bull, the Tattooed, the African. The assault rifle, the grenade, the war weapon replacing once and for all the knife or the box cutter. Violence, adrenaline, escape as your daily fix. A sadly typical and, in a way, very French pattern, in this section of France which the majority does not want to see. Until, one night, that disastrous exit from a service station shop somewhere in the Beauce region. The trial, the sentencing, and a couple of news reports on television. And then the prison cell. Time passing in slow motion, the desperately empty visiting room, the silence amid cries. The chaplain's visit once a week.

It wasn't so much a friendship between Kern and Djibril,

but rather a relationship of listeners with mutual respect, as though, during the course of his weekly visits, Kern had grasped the limits of his own experience. He didn't know much, and certainly no more than the man sitting opposite him, who had killed, had understood the immensity of his crime, and had the rest of a lifetime to regret it and forgive himself.

"I don't know, Djibril. I haven't thought of him in ages. Maybe you're right, maybe, in spite of myself, this boy reminds me of my brother; his bewilderment, the violence inside him, all hidden under the mask of an angel."

More than once, Kern had had the strange sense that he was the one more in need of confiding. That never happened to him with any of the other prisoners at Poissy. With the others, he'd listen, then speak, and a conversation might sometimes follow that would calm the atmosphere of the cells, so thick it was often difficult to breathe. Djibril's cell had the same atmosphere, the same everyday objects with which prisoners had to content themselves, the same obscene posters next to the same sentimental pictures cut out from the same magazines—except for one difference: there was a Dalloz penal code towering on one of Djibril's shelves, precariously balancing on a stack of law books and, on the small table, right next to the kettle, there was a wad of correspondence coursework. After a two-year basic qualification, the man sentenced to life was studying for a degree in law.

He gave Kern more coffee. "What this kid needs is for you to spare him the same end as your brother."

"Why do you think I come here every Thursday? I'm trying to spare you all from the same end as my brother!"

Kern drank his coffee in a single gulp. This time, he felt it burn him right through. "Sorry, I shouldn't have said that."

The prisoner laughed, then made the sign of the cross. "I absolve you, my son. But can you forgive yourself? For being alive, I mean, while your brother died alone in his cell?"

Kern made no reply, and Djibril stood up, his full stature towering over the small man. "Keep saying your prayers, François, but don't let that stop you from acting in order to avoid the worst. You can turn destiny around. By the time I understood that, it was far too late."

"I know. "

"You see, prison gives you time to think, to play the short movie of your life over and over again, and turn things around and around in your head in every direction. And to admit that there's no way to turn back."

"Yes, I know."

"You keep rehashing your thoughts. That's the real torture here: you keep going over your mistakes while you wait to drop dead. Like purgatory before hell."

Then he took the emaciated hand the priest was holding out to him in his huge paw. Kern felt a slight shudder. The prisoner had a much more concrete understanding of limbo than he, a priest, would ever have in his life, and he thought: In truth, I know nothing: he's the one with real knowledge.

"Thank you, Djibril."

"No problem. It's nice to feel useful. But don't let that make you forget to visit me. You know, if I don't have my little priest to talk to, I bottle up my anger and I start hitting my pals in the cafeteria. Over nothing. Over a piece of bread. Just to kill time. It's the survival of the fittest, and the fittest isn't always the most clever one or, as you'd say, the most Christian."

"In twenty-two years on the job, I've never heard such a string of nonsense."

Landard had just joined Gombrowicz in the corner of the office and was allowing himself another Gitane. It was about four in the afternoon. The attic room was sweltering, suffocating, and filled with an increasingly thick cloud of smoke every time Landard exhaled.

At the other end of the room, barely nine feet away, the blond angel, handcuffed to his chair, was now just a form lost in the fog. Landard carried on with his opinion. "The kid's a complete loon. Piece of cake for a court-appointed lawyer. I can already imagine the statement for the defense: 'My client is crazy, your Honor, his mother made him eat his poop when he was little, he pleads diminished responsibility.' And abracadabra, straight to the funny farm without needing to go through the prison stage. I'm telling you, Gombrowicz, the law is badly designed. It's not right this kind of freak should get a vacation on the house."

Landard went back to sit on the desk, while Gombrowicz got behind the computer.

"OK, Thibault, so we were talking about the procession."

"May I have a glass of water? I'm terribly thirsty."

"In a minute, Thibault, first the procession."

The young man appeared to search his memory, then asked, in his strange, rattling voice, "Procession?"

"Yes, the day before yesterday. The Assumption, remember? The Mass, the procession ..."

"The Assumption procession?"

"That's right, my boy. The statue of the Virgin, the priests, the Knights of the Holy-whatever, and the number in white who was wiggling her ass just a couple of yards away from you. Remember?"

"Yes, I remember, but your choice of words—"

"Did you know the girl, Thibault? Perhaps you can tell us her name."

"Never seen her before."

"Then why did you start hitting her?"

"If I told you, you wouldn't understand."

"Yes, but tell us anyway, and my colleague and I will do our best to understand."

The young man looked at Landard, then at Gombrowicz, then at Landard again. And a hint of a smile appeared on his lips despite the obvious stress caused by the interrogation.

"The Virgin Mary ordered me to."

Landard slapped himself on the thigh. "Fuck! Here we go again! The Virgin, the saints, and the little boy Jesus Christ."

"You see, you don't understand at all."

"Write it down, Gombrowicz, make sure you write it down: 'It's the Virgin Mary who ordered me to attack that young woman.' And do you happen to know why the good Virgin may have asked you to punish that pretty girl?"

"Not the faintest idea."

"Not the faintest—are you taking us for a ride, by any chance, Thibault? The Virgin Mary wouldn't have told you to give the girl a hammering the day before yesterday because she was a bit North African around the edges, would she, by any chance?"

Thibault walled himself up in a deep silence. Landard crushed his Gitane right under Gombrowicz's nose, in an ashtray overflowing with butts. The lieutenant, who was struggling to breathe and was beginning to sweat, grabbed it and emptied it in the garbage can with a sigh. That's when the young man started to speak again.

"I see what you're getting at. You're trying to accuse me of a racist attack. But the Virgin Mary isn't racist. How could she be? The Virgin Mary is a model to all the women in the world, whatever their skin color."

Landard felt the boy and his motive slipping away from him, so he raised his voice and brought his face a couple of inches away from the young man's. "Earlier, you told us that you were still living with your mother. In Saint-Cloud, right? How's your mom going to feel when she finds out that her son is suspected of killing a girl?"

The boy's breathing suddenly quickened. "My mother? What does my mother have to do with all this?"

"How's she going to feel, Thibault? Do you think she'll come to your trial? Do you think she'll bring you oranges when you're in Fleury prison?"

"Leave my mother alone. I didn't kill that girl."

"Then why did you hit her, Thibault? Tell me why."

Upset, Thibault started mumbling something, then, suddenly, the words crowded in his mouth and gushed out, like a powerful jet of water from a faucet because the washer's come loose. "Because she was a whore! Because she was mocking the Virgin Mary in her white dress. I hit her because she deserved it! Because she was strutting about before our very eyes in that provocative prostitute dress! I hit her to teach her a lesson! I hit her because she was asking for it! I hit her to urge her to be pure, humble, good, I hit her to urge her toward virginity!"

Thibault had off-loaded in spite of himself, and immediately seemed to regret it. He apologized for his choice of words. Opposite him, however, Captain Landard seemed suddenly filled with hot air, like a balloon, as though he was about to take off from the top of his desk.

"Write that down, Gombrowicz, 'I hit her to urge her toward virginity.'"

Gombrowicz was tapping away on his keyboard. He found the abrupt change of pace of the interrogation somewhat disturbing. Landard waited for the computer keys to stop rattling, then lit another cigarette and took a drag contentedly.

"Gombrowicz, will you call the little magistrate on her direct line, please?"

Once again, he leaned toward the suspect. "Tell me, Thibault. How about we take a little trip to your mother's to have a look inside your drawers? Do you think we'll be there before nine p.m.?"

He closed his door and double-locked it. He remained there for a moment, his forehead against the wood, his hand tense on the handle, listening for the city noises outside, which he could hear as though through a dense fog that had descended abundantly on this late afternoon of August 17th. In the street, a car drove by. The sound of a woman's footsteps. A child laughing. Then nothing.

He let go of the door handle, then went into the apartment, which was simple, bare, tidy, and where he had now been living for fifteen years. He abandoned his jacket on the back of a chair. Went to drink a glass of water. Or rather, he just filled it while staring at the clock on the white wall without really seeing it, for what might have been a long or a short time, standing there, holding the glass, before putting it down in the sink, still full.

He went into the bedroom, sat on the bed, looked at his hands, resting on his knees like a well-behaved child during the class photo, then stood up again and opened the closet in front of the bed. He took out a shoe box and placed it on a small table in the corner of the room, beneath a wooden crucifix nailed to the wall. He took an old Bayard alarm clock out of the box, then a magnifying glass, and an inkstained pencil case, and pulled open the zipper. There, he found pliers and four screwdrivers of different colors and sizes, which he lined up on both sides of the alarm clock. Finally, he took a black and white photo from the bottom of the box, and placed it in front of him, leaning it against the wall. He switched on a reading lamp fixed to the edge of the table, picked up the alarm clock in one hand and one of the four screwdrivers—the one with a faded red wooden handle—in the other. Slowly and with childlike application, he unscrewed the metal cover and finally opened it, revealing a mechanism that was at once basic and complex, as well as its manufacturing date: 1958. Then, with equal meticulousness, surrounded by a silence that was penetrated only by the sound of his breathing, and the faint ticking of the clock in the kitchen, he started taking the entire device apart.

A little before eight p.m., he put the two final pieces down in front of him. The entire alarm clock lay before him, in separate parts.

He was wearing a short-sleeved shirt. In the combination of daylight and lamplight, he saw that the red splotches had settled on his wrists and elbows. He could also feel them spreading under the table, on his calves, and up to his knees in this curious mixture of burning and itching he hadn't felt before. For the first time that evening, he looked away from his alarm clock and let his eyes linger on the photo propped up against the wall. Two boys, one about seven years old, the other perhaps ten, were standing with their arms around each other, staring into the lens, in a posture that evoked soccer players prior to a match. As a matter of fact, there was a ball on the ground, waiting for one of them—either the younger, small and dark, looking like a sickly chick, or the elder, blond and straight like wheat—to animate it with a powerful kick. The decor resembled that of a public school or an old-fashioned boarding school, with its paved courtyard surrounded by a high wall and, in the background, the corner of a single building whose only visible opening gave a glimpse of a stained glass window.

Once again, he put his hand into the shoe box and took out an old-fashioned-looking mercury thermometer. Still staring at the black and white photo, he slid the metal tip under his tongue and waited, motionless, in the fading light of the day that was slowly giving way to the cold, clinical glow of his reading lamp. Finally, he took it out of his mouth and read it: it was over a hundred and four. He placed the thermometer on the edge of the table.

Without a sound, without a sigh, Father Kern began putting his Bayard alarm clock with its 1958 mechanism back together.

Claire Kauffmann was hanging on to the roof strap. Her knees, which she kept close together, swayed left and right whenever the car swerved, and, with her left arm, she clutched against her chest the bag containing the Notre Dame file.

As they pulled up to a red light, Landard backtracked brusquely and the engine of the Peugeot 308 roared as he swerved to the right into a bus lane and drove toward the Seine without touching the brakes. He crossed Pont de Saint-Cloud at full speed. In the back seat, handcuffed and huddled against Gombrowicz, the blond angel sometimes looked at the road and sometimes into Landard's eyes, which he could see in the rearview mirror.

"Do you really think it's necessary to drive like this, captain? We'll easily be there before nine p.m. to start the search."

Landard turned on another burst of siren as they approached the bridge exit. "It's for the sake of the young man's mom, madame. I wouldn't like her to miss the start of her movie because of us. With a bit of luck we'll get there just after the news, while the commercials are on."

The magistrate rolled her eyes to the sky while the policeman stared at his suspect in the rearview mirror. "I bet your mom enjoys watching TV, doesn't she, Thibault? I bet she saw you come out of the cathedral on the one o'clock news. She must have thought, 'But that boy, there, with handcuffs and a jacket over his head, that's my boy!' Then she'll have watched the eight o'clock news just to make sure. Tell me, Thibault, do you think your mom will have recognized you despite the jacket over your head?"

Landard turned and repeated his question while looking his suspect straight in the eye. Gombrowicz, whose hamburger and fries were slowly finding their way back up, against all digestive logic, unclenched his teeth to admonish his superior. "*Putain*! Keep your eyes on the road, Landard, before you drive us into a lamp post!"

They drove around a line of cars entering the westbound highway and headed toward Saint-Cloud. A few minutes later, they stopped, straddling the sidewalk, outside a 1970s building. White as a sheet and his face glowing with sweat, Gombrowicz got the blond angel out of the car, holding his arm, while Landard was already walking into the building, closely followed by Claire Kauffmann.

In the elevator, they refrained from talking, the four of them crammed like sardines in a can. Claire Kauffmann could smell the odor of cold tobacco absorbed by Captain's Landard's jacket, and the scent of cheap deodorant wafting from Lieutenant Gombrowicz's moist armpits. She could also hear the young suspect's breathing quickening as they rose and drew closer to his mother's door.

A little woman in a robe, with thinning hair and a stooped, sickly form, opened the door. When she saw her handcuffed son, she began to moan, her eyes wide and panic-stricken. With a hand deformed by arthritis, she covered her mouth, which was wide with surprise. She would not close it again—or barely—for the rest of the search.

What struck Claire Kauffmann when she first walked into the hallway was the stuffy smell: How long had it been since the windows had been opened? The blinds were closed. By the window, she noticed that strips of wide, brown Scotch tape had been stuck over the Venetian blinds, preventing light and air from coming in between the slats. A glance around the place informed her that all the other openings in the apartment had suffered the same treatment. The blond angel and his mother lived in a veritable tomb consisting of a kitchen, a bathroom, two bedrooms, and a small living room.

An old-looking television set was blasting a commercial for an insurance company. Landard had estimated the time of his arrival well. "Is Thibault's father not here, madame?"

"He passed away, inspector. He died twenty-one years ago, in a car accident on the road to Satory. He was a soldier. I was six months pregnant when it happened. Thibault never knew his father." She turned to her son and put her fist in front of her mouth again. "Thibault ... The police ... What have you done now?"

Claire Kauffmann pulled the file out of her bag. "Madame, your son has been arrested as part of a murder investigation. He will remain in custody until noon tomorrow, unless his custody is extended by twenty-four hours. These police officers are here to search your son's room in order to help their investigation. Do we have your permission?"

"Good Lord! Thibault! So it was you on TV. It was you at Notre Dame. What have you done now?"

"Will you permit us to see your son's room, madame?"

With a hesitant hand gesture, she showed them a door at the end of the corridor. Landard headed there first, walking along walls with faded wallpaper patterned with flowers that seemed to have wilted years earlier. Touching the door handle, he turned to the young suspect, whose arm Gombrowicz was still holding.

"All right, Thibault, my boy? Do you mind if we take a look? Now do pay attention to where we search and what we take away because at the end you'll have to sign a little piece of paper for us. All right?"

He leaned on the handle and opened the door. Inside, there was the same stifling air as in the rest of the apartment. Landard groped for the switch on the wall. Once the light was on, he couldn't stop himself from swearing.

The young man then entered, followed by Gombrowicz and Claire Kauffmann. The magistrate and the two policemen stood for a moment, taken aback, their eyes sliding along the walls, shelves, cupboard, and display cabinets. Gombrowicz, who'd turned even paler because of the lack of oxygen in the place, turned to his superior. "Honestly, Landard, have you ever seen anything like it?"

The blond angel's room was a veritable museum devoted to the Blessed Virgin Mary. Lined up against walls papered with the same wilted floral pattern, from floor to ceiling and everywhere in between, there were statuettes of all shapes and sizes that seemed to be watching the three visitors with searching eyes. In the few unoccupied gaps on the shelves, childlike drawings, framed under glass, had been fixed to the wall. They all had the same subject: Mary, in all her forms, all her representations, was ever-present and celebrated.

One picture in particular caught Gombrowicz's attention, perhaps because the drawing was more imposing than the others, or because it was the only one in color, or perhaps because it had been hung opposite the bed. It was a Virgin Mary wearing a crown, her skin deathly pale, surrounded by red and blue angels, holding a ruddy, chubby-cheeked baby Jesus on her left knee. There was something chillingly erotic about the drawing, not just because of the Virgin's beautiful face, but because her left breast was protruding from her bodice, and that breast, rounded, full and extremely pale, drew the eye more than anything else in the drawing.

"Beautiful, isn't she? It's a fifteenth-century French painting. I had to go all the way to Antwerp to see it. It took me three days to reproduce it. Remember, Mom?"

Without looking away from the drawing, Gombrowicz gave a whistle of admiration. "Did you do this? And all the other things on the wall?"

In a voice that was suddenly more confident, the young man's mother answered instead of him. "Thibault's drawings are extraordinary, inspector. He's working toward getting into the École des Beaux-Arts."

"Mom!"

"You'll get into the Beaux-Arts, my son, I'm sure of it. And through your art you'll celebrate faith in Mary and Jesus Christ."

Landard, who'd already opened the only cupboard in the room and was in the process of emptying its drawers, suddenly pulled out a stack of sketches and waved them over his head. "What about these, Thibault? Are they also for the Beaux-Arts?"

He laid out the sheets of paper on the bed one by one, and his suspect's face gradually dropped as he lined up a series of pornographic sketches featuring a Virgin Mary with full lips, her dress pulled up, wearing fishnet tights and stilettos, and spreading her legs to reveal her most intimate parts.

"If you don't mind, Thibault, I'm putting these in my favorite order. Is that all right? Ladies and gentlemen, look here carefully. The first masterpiece produced by our friend Thibault in anticipation of his admission to the Beaux-Arts Academy: The Virgin gently masturbates and finally reaches ecstasy. Very beautiful, very pure. Still, there's a soupçon of Saint Theresa about it. Be careful about getting your saints mixed up, Thibault, otherwise, there's no Beaux-Arts this year. Second masterpiece in anticipation of Thibault's admission into the Beaux-Arts: In order to preserve her precious virginity, naughty Mary pleasures herself in the behind with the help of a ... a ... What is it you've stuck up your Virgin Mary's ass, Thibault? Gombrowicz? Your opinion? Madame? Any idea? Never mind. Let's proceed with the visit."

Claire Kauffmann was increasingly uncomfortable as the grotesque exhibition went on. She was slightly dizzy and felt the blood draining from her head. Was it the lack of air in this hermetically sealed room? Was it the obviously sadistic pleasure Landard took in humiliating his suspect? Was it the mask of shame Thibault wore on his face? His mother's severe expression? Or did the obscene sketches drawn by this libidinous teenager propel her back to memories that were older, more painful, more personal?

Gombrowicz, who had laughed at the first drawing, was not laughing anymore. A vaguely complicit smile had lasted for a moment but now it had vanished, and his sad, uneasy eyes were now darting from his boss to the sketches, then from the sketches to his boss.

Still, Landard carried on with a glee he was not expressing by chance. From the moment of the arrest, he had gathered that the suspect's weak spot was his relationship with his mother. He managed more or less to keep to the same version of the events with the police, but Landard sensed that, in the presence of his mother, he was a vulnerable child at the mercy of a terrible judgment, bordering on panic. So he laid it on thick until the very last drawing, the one that obviously interested him most for his investigation.

"You must have guessed—you must have—which one I've chosen to complete the exhibition, Thibault. Look carefully, ladies and gentlemen, the masterpiece above all masterpieces, the major component of this cabinet of curiosities of my friend Thibault. Look carefully. This is what we're going to call it: giving in to her dirtiest urges, hot Mary stuffs hot wax up her fanny." Landard clapped. "My dear members of the Beaux-Arts judging panel, I would like to give a Special Mention to young Thibault in the religious pornography category. If the panel doesn't agree, speak loud and clear now, or forever hold your peace."

Almost simultaneously, Lieutenant Gombrowicz and Deputy Magistrate Kauffmann felt the irrepressible urge to go out, to leave this unbreathable air, he in order to find a toilet and finally free his stomach of the burger and fries that had been torturing him for an least an hour; she—in order to crack open the nearest window in the living room. The faint draft that filtered through the sealed blinds did her a world of good, and Claire Kauffmann remained like this, holding the window handle, pressing her forehead against the blind.

"My son has been taking refuge in religion for a long time, mademoiselle. For the past year or so his piety has been bordering on obsession. I've hardly seen him since the summer. He spends all day in Notre Dame. And yet trust me, mademoiselle, Thibault is not a murderer."

Claire Kauffmann took one last breath of oxygen, and turned to the suspect's mother. "You must admit that your son has an odd concept of religion, madame, and a very dirty concept of women."

Thibault's mother lowered her head and Claire Kauffmann, irritated by her silence, decided to start her interrogation. "What time did he come home on Sunday night? Do you remember?"

"I go to bed at around eight. You see, I'm sick. I guess sorrow's been eating away at me all these years. The death of my husband. I'm scared of everything. I don't dare go out anymore. I get vertigo. Mademoiselle, if only you knew the kind of life I've had since my husband's death. Raising a boy on my own, you know. You're so attractive. Do you have children?"

"Consequently, you didn't hear your son come back in, right? Not even a vague recollection? A sound ... Something ... Please try to remember. It could be very important."

She looked at her with a lost, distraught expression that was an evident plea: What must I say to prove that my son is innocent? At what time must he have come home on Sunday night in order to be cleared once and for all?

However, all that came from her lips was an inaudible whisper that turned into a sob.

At the end of the corridor, Thibault was sitting on his bed, his face buried in his adolescent hands, surrounded by his madman's pornography in black pencil. Landard put a finger on his shoulder. "Come on, Thibault, let's go back to prison. You'll spend the night there and you can sleep on it. You've got a decision to make, my boy. Tomorrow morning we'll have another talk, you and I. Then we'll take you before a committing magistrate and you'll have to be a bit more talkative than you've been today. Do you understand what I'm saying? It's crunch time, Thibault. You really don't have a choice now, so you'd better spit it out. Gombrowicz, put the cuffs back on. Let's see what the magistrate's up to and go home."

Gombrowicz leaned over the young man to cuff him. That was when he noticed, concealed behind the headboard, a switch that looked very homemade. He signaled to Landard with his chin. The captain reached out to the wall, but the blond angel immediately stopped him with his high-pitched voice. "Don't touch that. You hear me? I forbid you to touch that! I forbid you to touch that switch."

"As if I'm going to stand on ceremony here, Thibault. Gombrowicz, get ready. You never know."

Suddenly tense from adrenalin, Gombrowicz placed a hand on the service weapon at his belt. Landard counted to three as the young man's protestations grew louder, then pushed the switch. The room was plunged into a darkness made total by the thick Scotch tape over the blinds. Gombrowicz slowly pulled his weapon out of its holster.

"Landard? Fuck, Landard, what's going on?"

Before his superior could speak, Gombrowicz got the answer. In the impenetrable darkness around them all, the three or four hundred Virgins lining the shelves suddenly started flashing in unison, turning the room into a carnival fun house.

Facedown on his bed, Thibault was crying in the blinking light. In between sobs, he let out two childish syllables which he seemed ready to repeat for the rest of the night, "Mommy ... Mommy ..."

WEDNESDAY

HE HAD COME IN THROUGH THE PORTAL OF SAINT ANNE ALONG with the first tourists of the day, with his customary camouflage-patterned bag over one shoulder and wearing, as he did every day of the year, in winter as well as in summer, his most valuable possession: a torn, filthy, wine-colored padded jacket that was constantly shedding feathers on the stone floor, allowing him to be tracked, so to speak.

Once inside, he kneeled right in the middle of the narthex, directly in line with the central aisle near the western entrance, and crossed himself. He mumbled something into his long, blond, tousled beard, then got up again, clumsily, his left side dragged down by the weight of his bag and, since it was after 8 o'clock in the morning, a state of advanced drunkenness. Having more or less managed to pull himself up, he turned right toward the south pillar, where there was an embedded font that was three-quarters full. Then, with obsessive—almost coquettish—care, he dipped his fingers into the holy water and began washing inside his ears.

"Krzysztof! Krzysztof, what are you doing? Not in the font, please. Have you really nowhere else to wash? What about the fountain in the square? For heaven's sake, Krzysztof!"

Krzysztof apologized in an incomprehensible blend of Polish and French, picked up his bag and headed for the exit. A few steps farther, however, he seemed to think better of it, looked around, somewhat disorientated, stared at the man who had gently chided him, and finally recognized Father Kern. Then his face, weary from drink and lack of sleep, lit up and he immediately approached, hammering the four points of the cross on his chest with fingers thick as sausages.

"I tell you! I see! I tell!"

Krzysztof divided his time between the Polish Catholic Mission in the 18th arrondissement and the cathedral of Notre Dame, where he'd now been coming for three years. Here, he found some warmth in the winter and some coolness in the summer. He would usually sit in a corner by himself and spend the whole day sleeping, his large, blond head rocking up and down in fits and starts, as he woke up and dozed off. Sometimes, he would take a seat beneath the large crucified Christ on the south side, near the jar, on one of the chairs reserved for the worshippers waiting their turn to confess. However, Krzysztof smelled very bad and his odor, a blend of grime and rancid alcohol, would chase away every last candidate for forgiveness. The latter, queasy and indignant, never failed to warn one of the cathedral guards who then had the task of removing Krzysztof from the building with a gentle but firm hand, protected, just in case, by a antibacterial latex glove. Invariably, Krzysztof would start shouting in that blend of languages only he knew, arguing that he had as much right to confess as the others, or to pray, or to sleep in peace slap bang in the middle of the cathedral. And the more he shouted, the more he was surrounded by guards—gloved, too—who would appear, as though by magic, from behind the pillars, and escort him to his principal place of residence: Square Jean-XXIII, which separated Notre Dame from the Seine and where every night, after avoiding the rounds of a member of staff of the municipal gardens, he unrolled his sleeping bag and lay down to sleep.

Only once had Krzysztof dared go into the actual jar. Father Kern, who was on duty that day, had, contrary to custom, left the door open and switched on the fan built into the stained glass window of the chapel, in order to create a draft, then had taken the time to hear Krzysztof's story—without understanding much of it—from his native Poland to the streets of Paris after quite a few detours, binges, and fights. Krzysztof had been grateful to him ever since.

Krzysztof wasn't mean. Only alcohol could make him a little aggressive, but seldom so, and his bouts of bad temper then made him look like a large bear dressed in a grimy red padded jacket. He would generally calm down as quickly as he'd flared up, looking around as he had just done with Father Kern, suddenly remembering he was in a church. And a church, he knew since his childhood in the outskirts of Kraków, was a place reserved for calm and prayer. A place from which shouts and alcohol must be banned; a place where violence, murder, and death had no place either.

"I tell you, I see! I know!"

"What do you know, Krzysztof? What do you want to tell me?"

"Girl! I see!"

"What girl, Krzysztof?"

"Girl in white!"

Father Kern took the Polish vagrant aside and gestured at him to keep his bear's voice down.

"When did you see her, Krzysztof? Try to remember. Which day and at what time?"

"*W niedzielę, wieczorem.*"

"I can't understand what you're saying. Was it Sunday? Sunday night?"

"*Tak*. Sunday."

"What time?"

Krzysztof did not understand the question, so Father Kern pointed at his watch. Krzysztof opened his arms in a gesture of powerlessness and also pointed at his bare wrist, deprived of a watch.

"*W nocy.*"

"At night? Is that right, Krzysztof? Was it already nighttime when you came across her?"

"*Tak. W nocy.*"

"Tell me, Krzysztof. Where did you see her? Was she alone? What was she doing exactly?"

Krzysztof made a huge effort to remember. Despite the tiredness, despite the alcohol, despite the thousand difficulties he'd had to tackle since that already seemingly distant Sunday night in order to find food, drink, a place to sleep, and avoid fights, he made an effort to search his memory, and somehow or other managed to put some order in his thoughts. However, just as he was about to convey them, he collided head on with the language barrier. Father Kern was growing impatient. Krzysztof tried to express himself through gestures but his large paws also remained silent.

"Never mind, Krzysztof. Tell me in your own language. You never know, perhaps I'll understand one or two words. Let's try."

Krzysztof took a deep breath then, in an overpoweringly alcoholic whisper, he began. "In garden. I go to sleep, much plants— *schowany za roślinami*. I see back of *katedra. Zauważyłem dziewczynę*—girl—open gate from street. She have code for *kłódki. Ona weszła do ogrodu*. Into garden. White, white. All white. She look—*Wyglądała pięknie w świetle gwiazd.* Stairs, she goes up, knock on door. Back of *katedra.* Door opens, she go inside. *Nie wiem, co zdarzyło się później.*"

Father Kern his eyes to the tall vaults, darkened day after day, month after month, year after year, by the sour breath of hundreds of thousands of visitors. He murmured, "Pray for us poor sinners." He murmured, "Sin has penetrated these walls. It didn't have to come in through the keyhole because it simply had the key." And then he murmured again, "This is the meaning of Your sign, O Lord. You have plunged me into darkness in order to push me to find the path of light again. You've put the key to the sin into the palm of my hand in order to test my faith. It's up to me to find out which door it opens. It's up to me to discover the identity of the killer."

Looking at the small priest absorbed in his Low Mass, the Polish vagrant, wrapped up in his grimy padded jacket, wondered what all that gibberish was about.

"Luna Hamache. Twenty-one years old, born in Paris, in the eighteenth arrondissement. Studying history at the Villetaneuse university. Living with her parents in Rue Guy-Môquet. Father of Algerian origin, unemployed, mother a care worker in Beaujon. Does that ring any bells, Thibault?"

"No. Who is it?"

"It's the girl who was strangled on Sunday night right in the middle of *Rejoice, Mary.* Her father recognized her picture in yesterday's *Le Parisien.* Not easy finding out about your daughter's death by opening a paper on the counter of a café, right, Thibault?

"Yes, it's terrible."

"Terrible? Do you know where her parents are right now? They're at Forensics, in the process of identifying a corpse pulled out of a drawer. Don't you think it's time you started being a bit more talkative, Thibault?"

"But I told you, I didn't do anything to that poor girl."

"Didn't do anything? You're kidding, right? We've got about fifty witnesses who saw you hitting that poor girl, as you say, during the procession. And less than five hours later, while the movie session was in full swing in Notre Dame, someone squeezed her neck so tight, she jumped so far out of her skin she landed in heaven. You'll excuse me if we have good reason to believe that the sicko who did her in is you, Thibault."

"You have no proof."

"We'll have proof enough in less than two hours. And you know why, Thibault? Because in less than two hours, the medical examiner will have finished his postmortem report. In your opinion, whose DNA are we going to find on the poor girl's clothes? As far as I'm concerned, I'm not too bothered about proof, especially given the porn drawings we found at your place. What I would like to know, however, is why. Why and how?"

"Ask the murderer. It's got nothing to do with me."

"I'm going to tell you what happened. I'm going to tell you exactly. On Sunday, you went to the cathedral like you always do on the day of the Assumption. Like every year, you had your crucifix in one hand and your dick in the other, if you'll excuse the expression, so to speak."

"Honestly, inspector, do you have to use that kind of language?"

"The Day of the Assumption is a bit like New Year's Day for fetishists of the Virgin Mary. Right, Thibault? It's the only day of the year when they get the silver statue out. Wipe it off a bit and off we go on a little tour of Paris. Knights, priests, the old pious folks, everyone follows. And among all that crowd, there's also degenerates like you who take pictures while waiting to go back home and jerk off all night. Right, Thibault?"

"I don't know."

"Right, now wait, I haven't finished my story. Imagine that in the middle of the procession, you come across a second Virgin Mary who looks like the twin of your statue, except that this one isn't made of silver but flesh and blood, all dressed in white, like the one at Lourdes, except that she's a bit of a streetwalker type, miniskirt and nice tits, you know who I mean?"

"I think so, yes."

"And the girl has the right, after all, to air her little ass—after all, shit, this is France, not Saudi Arabia!—and so she excites you so much that you suddenly think in that disgusting little head of yours: fuck, she'd better stop prick-teasing like that, or I'm really going to lose it. So you start hitting her like a punching bag, isn't that true, Thibault? You hit her until she's bleeding, until my pal Mourad intervenes with all the subtlety he's famous for. Am I not right so far, Thibault? Isn't that exactly what happened?"

"That doesn't prove anything."

"So then you leave and go for a walk until the evening. And then, at about nine or ten, you're horny again. You need to go and see your Virgin Mary on the big screen. Who knows? Maybe you can even touch yourself a couple of times in the dark. And who should you see, right there in the darkness, in the middle of Notre Dame? Our pretty little thing in a miniskirt. In the dark, you can see nothing but her. I swear she glows in the dark in her white dress, just like an apparition. Right, Thibault? So you wait awhile, you wait for her to get up and go for a stroll, light a candle by some statue or other in a dark corner, and then you pounce on her. And you know what happens next, Thibault? The

stupid fool starts screaming. She tries to call for help. So you put
your hand over her mouth, your hand over her nose, and then
you start panicking. Of course, *Rejoice, Mary* is blasting from the
movie speakers at full volume. But even so, she keeps wriggling
around, right, Thibault? So then what do you do? You put your
arm around her neck and you pull, you squeeze, you crush as
hard as you can. Until your madonna isn't moving anymore.
She's still, totally still, and beautiful, still and beautiful like a
statue. Tell me, Thibault, tell me that's how it happened."

"It's not true, inspector. Your story's completely off base."

"You and your mother are beginning to seriously piss me off
with this 'inspector' business. This isn't Inspector Maigret! It's
'captain!' From now on you call me 'captain!'"

"All right, captain."

"And what happened next? You let them lock you in? Did
you hide deep inside one of the chapels with the dead girl in
your arms and wait for the cathedral to close? Is that it? You were
lucky, you know, Thibault, lucky Mourad didn't do his rounds
that night. Once you were alone with her, you had all the time
you wanted to do all that disgusting stuff with the wax. You had
all the time in the world to redo her virginity with candles. It's
so much more reassuring for lunatics like you, isn't it—a woman
reduced to the state of a statue, white, virgin, dead, who you can't
do anything to anymore. A relic. Nothing left to do but worship
her. And then what? What happened? You calmly waited for the
cathedral to reopen in the morning, did you? Is that it? You went
out whistling a happy tune, finally calmed down, your hands in
your pockets. Is that it?"

"I don't know. I wasn't there. I was in bed asleep."

"You're really starting to tick me off, Thibault. Let's see how
clever you are later, in front of the committing magistrate."

"What time is it?"

"Why do you want to know?"

"No reason."

"What time is it, Gombrowicz?"

"It's after eleven."

"What's the smile for?"

"You can only keep me in custody for another hour."

"You think we're going to let you go?"

"Twenty-four hours, captain. It's the law."

"You wait and see, Thibault. Here, when we like people, we have the right to keep them a little longer. I hope you like your room and your roommates at the prison, because you might just have to spend another night there. Gombrowicz? Call the little magistrate for me, will you?"

He had formed an opinion about their methods. The violence with which he'd seen them arrest their suspect in the glass confessional had inspired in him nothing but fear and contempt. Would Krzysztof, for whom anyone in a uniform was suspect and possibly an enemy, agree to speak to them? Would he repeat what he'd seen in the garden behind the cathedral the night of the murder? The chances were very slim. Nonexistent, in fact. It was quite possible the Polish vagrant would go elsewhere, clear out from the neighborhood of Notre Dame at the slightest prospect of a confrontation with the police, and never reappear.

What could he do? Where could he go? Whom should he talk to? Ever since he'd been chaplain at Poissy, he'd learned to handle this huge machine with caution: French Justice, with its apparently noble goals, its necessary role, but which changed faces depending on who was standing before it. He needed to find the right person to speak to, knock on the right door. The fate of the blond young man, the one they had handcuffed before his eyes and those of Christ, might depend on it.

Father Kern avoided the sacristy and left directly through the door of Saint-Étienne, on the side of the Seine. He walked along the side of the cathedral, past the presbytery, where the rector lived, and looked up at the windows of his apartment. There was no rush to tell him. Besides, he didn't know what to tell him exactly. Should he mention Krzysztof? And this almost miraculous translation from Polish into French he seemed to have been granted? Strangely, Kern was hesitant about sharing that experience, even with another priest at the cathedral. And yet he was spoiled for choice. Notre Dame had about twenty permanent priests—canons, chaplains, reception priests, student priests—not counting visiting parish priests from France or abroad who came to fill in during the summer. With some of them, Kern had formed bonds that went beyond the spiritual and the professional. A rapport of true friendship had been established. Yet at this precise stage on his path through the cathedral, he chose to take pleasure in a kind of solitude, laden with an as yet imperceptible weight, but which he knew would grow heavier in the hours to come.

He went through the gate that separated him from the square. He walked straight ahead, with a step he hoped was confident but which, yard by yard, was actually becoming more and more undecided.

He stopped right in the middle of the large square, staring at the ground, and was immediately accosted by a Roma beggar woman who held out a frayed postcard on which a no-less frayed appeal for generosity was written. She asked him to help feed her baby, she asked him for money to help her handicapped brother, her bedridden mother. He looked at the plastic sandals and the overly long toenails that had just come into his field of vision, then raised his head and studied the young woman. Under her tousled mop of hair, she had extraordinarily beautiful green eyes. She lowered them and noticed, pinned to his lapel, the small metal cross, the only distinctive sign of his priesthood. She knew only too well that the priests of Notre Dame were generally not the type who put their hands in their pockets in order to finance Romanian charities. Realizing her mistake, she laughed, revealing a set of teeth with a metallic gleam. Father Kern smiled back at her and resumed his walk.

A little farther, he was approached by another woman begging. This one was not from Romania but from the national radio. She held out a rectangle of card with her name printed under the Radio France logo. She asked if he'd witnessed the suspect's arrest the day before. She asked him for his testimony, and whether the young man in custody was a regular at Notre Dame. He stared at the mic she was holding out to him and replied that all interviews had to be applied for at the cathedral press office. Then he said good-bye to her with a brief nod, and walked away.

He went down Quai du Marché-Neuf, walking against the traffic. He passed the police prefecture on his right, crossed Boulevard du Palais, and stopped once again, a small, motionless figure, lost in the constant flow of visiting tourists. Ahead of him began Quai des Orfèvres. Number 36 was about a hundred yards away. He stuffed his two fists in the pockets of his jacket. With his left hand, he felt the pipe and tobacco pouch he always carried with him. He approached the parapet of Pont Saint-Michel, put his packet of Peterson on it, and began stuffing his pipe while watching the Seine flow by. Below, a *bateau-mouche* was about to pass under the bridge. From the top gallery of the boat, a little blond girl waved at him. Father Kern responded slightly late, after the child had already disappeared behind the pier of the bridge. He lit his pipe and allowed the taste and smell of tobacco to permeate his nose, mouth, and throat.

He thought about Djibril, and the fate he was now unable to change behind the walls of his prison. He thought of the advice the murderer had given him: pray, yes, but also act before it was too late, act while you still have the freedom of choice and action. Finally, he thought about his brother. To act, act before death comes for us, act before we turn to dust. Act before we're buried under regrets and shovelfuls of soil.

He put his pouch back into his left pocket and, followed by a trail of fragrant smoke that escaped intermittently from his pipe, he turned right in the direction of the Palais.

The morning court session had ended with a flourish, with the case of a thirty-eight-year-old tile installer. The night before, in an advanced state of drunkenness, he'd hit his wife with a hammer in front of their three children aged twelve, ten, and seven. She was currently in the hospital with a fractured shoulder blade. When Claire Kauffmann asked him the reasons for his act, the man, sitting opposite her in the tiny defendant's box, had at first shrugged before answering, "Tiredness."

The deputy magistrate had slammed shut the file with the police report before suggesting an immediate trial.

With her heavy load of papers in the crook of her arm, she went along the endless corridors of the Palais de Justice, climbed steps in every direction, walked through creaking doors, along flaking walls, picking up along the way hastily scribbled bits of paper or Post-it notes that had fallen off doors they'd been stuck on in order to indicate that such-and-such a judge or such-and-such a deputy had been moved elsewhere owing to lack of space or funds. She passed clerks of court, magistrates, and police; defendants who looked distraught, lost in this neon-lit labyrinth where even professionals sometimes struggled to find their bearings, some of them handcuffed and kept on a leash by a gendarme, their staring eyes expressing the boredom, the anxiety, and the tiredness of a night spent in the Palais cells.

She went to her office to put down her stack of files, and immediately grabbed that of young Thibault, the suspect in the Notre Dame murder case, whose twenty-four-hour custody was about to expire and needed to be urgently renewed. As she was going back out, the telephone rang. Her fellow deputy picked up while Claire Kauffmann paused in the doorway. "It's Reception on the Boulevard du Palais side," she said. "Apparently there's a priest from the cathedral who wants to speak with you."

"Later," she replied. "Give him my direct line and ask him to call back in two hours' time."

Then she left, the file in the crook of her arm, walking in small, quick, high-heeled steps toward the Crime Squad, where Captain Landard and the alleged murderer were waiting for her.

Once in the room, she felt nauseous. The air was unbreathable and the cloud of smoke so thick, she guessed rather than saw that Landard was sitting, as usual, on the corner of his desk. Opposite him, handcuffed to his chair, the suspect seemed to be staring at the policeman's shoes. Landard got up and went to the deputy magistrate. For a moment, they stood by the door, speaking in hushed tones.

"Is this a new interrogation technique, captain? Do you smoke your suspects like herrings?"

"Absolutely, Mademoiselle Kauffmann. At night, we marinate them in the humid basement of the cells. During the day, we smoke them under the fourth-floor roof. We alternate chill with stifling heat. A little combination that's already yielded results.

The prisoners come out of it—how shall I put it?—softer, wiser, more inclined to talk."

"Seriously, captain, may I open the window? You can't breathe here."

"If you insist. It's a whole atmosphere I'm only going to have to reconstruct once your charming form is out of here."

"Where's Lieutenant Gombrowicz?"

"Down in the courtyard. I sent him out to have his sandwich. Shall we get on with it, madame? Shall we give our little blond angel a second round?"

"Don't call him that, captain."

"Does it bother you?"

"You know as well as I do that there's nothing angelic about this young man."

"No need to get all hot and bothered. It's just a friendly little nickname."

"I'm tired of people giving affectionate nicknames to perverts, you see? I'm tired of rapists being described as libertines or seducers. I'm tired of innuendos like 'But what was she doing in the guy's apartment at that time of night?' I'm tired of gentle euphemisms violent husbands use to explain why they've sent their wives to Emergency. I'm tired of hearing 'Of course I didn't hit her. It was just a couple of slaps to calm her down.' In our profession, words are important, captain, words have meaning, they have weight. The terms rape and murder have legal consequences, and I find it especially tendentious that a professional like yourself should call a defendant suspected of sexual assault and murder a 'little blond angel.' Have you got the form ready?"

Landard gave the deputy magistrate his seat behind the desk. She opened the window wide, sat down opposite Thibault, and studied him carefully. There was nothing angelic about him except the nickname. The night he'd spent in the cells had visibly overwhelmed and broken him. Landard was laying siege to a fortress that was ready to yield. If the young man had something on his conscience, it would take less than an hour to make him confess.

"Young man, I've come to inform you that your custody is being prolonged by another twenty-four hours."

The boy was still staring at the spot on the side of the desk left vacant by the captain's shoes. He had not paid the deputy magistrate the slightest attention.

"Did you hear me? Are you all right?"

Without stirring, without even blinking, he began to talk, and Claire Kauffmann was suddenly struck by how very pale he was.

"They went to see my mother, madame. They went to see her and they made her talk. Then they showed her on their screens like a circus animal, her face streaming with tears, with more wrinkles than a mummy. They showed my mother in tears on TV to millions of viewers."

Claire Kauffmann turned to the police officer. "What's he saying? What's he talking about?"

"Didn't you watch it? They interviewed his mother, and showed it on the one o'clock news."

"You're joking! Which station? Who told them the identity of the suspect?"

"No idea, madame. I guess they found out, they were doing their jobs, just like you and me."

"And who showed him the interview?"

"We had a little break during our chat, about ten minutes ago. Gombrowicz clearly needed some fresh air, so I sent him downstairs and Thibault quietly watched the news while we were waiting for you, just like an old couple over a TV dinner."

At the mention of the television report, the young man sud-

denly looked dizzy. Claire Kauffmann walked around the desk
and put a hand on his shoulder. "Captain, remove his handcuffs."

"That's not very prudent, madame."

"Captain Landard, I'm asking you to remove his handcuffs
immediately. I'm calling a doctor."

Landard complied, let the deputy magistrate do as she saw
fit, and, hands in his pockets, went and stood comfortably at
the other end of the room. She picked up the receiver. While
the number was ringing, she turned again to the young man.
He finally raised his eyes, which had been totally emptied of
everything, toward the young woman, and she noticed for the
first time how pale his eyes were, an almost translucent gray, a
gray like tracing paper, as if they were only slightly masking the
inside of his soul. He joined his hands, which were now free,
and recited in a whisper: Hail Mary full of grace, the Lord is
with thee. Blessed art thou among women, and blessed be the
fruit of thy womb, Jesus. Holy Mary, Mother of God, pray for
us sinners. Now, and at the hour of our death.

Then he stood up and ran.

Deputy Kauffmann's phone had now been ringing in vain for
three hours. Father Kern had never considered it important to
get himself a cell phone, a quirk he now bitterly regretted, forced
as he now was to leave his jar between confessions to go to the
antediluvian pay phone in the sacristy, which nobody had used
since the advent of mobile phones. In order to reach the device,
which had been stuffed at the end of the corridor linking the
cathedral and the sacristy, he had to go all around the ambulatory
through the north side, so as to avoid at all costs the south end,
where, as usual, Madame Pipi had parked her behind and her

flowery hat for the day. A little earlier in the afternoon, as Kern was walking across the cathedral between two attempts to reach the Palais de Justice, he'd caught the eye of the old lady with the hat, and her expression was even more raving mad than usual, as though a flow of anguish was about to burst out, a torrent, a scream about to explode any moment now amid worshippers and tourists. Kern had decided to make a detour, struggling to look away from the glistening eyes staring at him from beneath the plastic poppies, since he considered his phone call to Claire Kauffmann to be more urgent than Madame Pipi's confessions.

However, once he'd reach the pay phone, he'd still have to wait to be alone, wait for the sacristan to go and polish the silver in some other distant corner of the cathedral, wait for the duty guard to finish his break and his coffee—since the staff coffee machine was in the sacristy—wait for a worshipper coming to ask for a few drops of holy water for her sick relative to leave, the precious liquid lapping at the bottom of a plastic bottle. And when the coast was finally clear, it was always the same reply he heard on the line: a tone that was becoming increasingly irritating and gave the impression that the entire Palais de Justice had been evacuated as the result of a bomb explosion.

It was now past four o'clock. Father Kern hung up the receiver again, promising himself to try his luck once more in a few minutes. Like the day before, he could feel his temperature rising, and this only increased his double feeling of urgency and nervousness. He would leave early, this evening; his night, he knew already, did not bode well.

He sat down on one of the wooden chests in the corridor of the sacristy. The stained glass windows of the Chapter cloister spread a green-tinted light on his back. Nearby, on the right-hand side, behind the leather-lined door between him and the cathedral, the anonymous mass of tourists emitted a dull hubbub worthy of the Tower of Babel, which echoed endlessly, from morning till night, beneath the vaults of the great aisle.

Father Kern looked at his watch and went toward the pay phone, but was immediately interrupted by Mourad, the guard, who had come in by the external door that gave onto the presbytery. The two men looked at each other for a moment, both embarrassed by each other's presence, then Mourad greeted the priest with a weary gesture and disappeared into the sacristy. Kern sat back down. He would have to wait again before he could phone.

He heard the rumble of the coffee machine. Shortly afterward, Mourad reappeared, holding a plastic cup. He collapsed more than sat on the other end of the carved chest on which the priest was already sitting. They remained there for a moment, in the relative silence of this corridor, which was disturbed by Mourad's repetitive sighs and the sound of the plastic stirrer at the bottom of his cup. Father Kern began to stuff his pipe.

"You don't look too well, Mourad. Something not right?"

"Not right, Father, not right at all."

"What's going on? Tell me."

"An injustice, Father, that's what's going on. An injustice like I've never known in my whole life."

"You've just come from the presbytery, haven't you?"

"That's right, Father."

"Did you go and see the rector?"

"That's right, Father. A little earlier, I got a call on my walkie-talkie, 'Mourad, the rector wants to see you.' You know, Father, we don't get summoned up there often."

"I know."

"So I go up to the presbytery as fast as I can, knock, and walk into the rector's office. You'll never guess what he wanted to talk to me about."

Father Kern took the time to light his pipe before replying. Heavy, fragrant curls of smoke rose above his head. "It was about your rounds last Sunday night, wasn't it?"

The guard sat up straight on the chest. "Good grief, does everybody here know?! Everybody in the world seems to know that I didn't do my rounds after closing! Everybody except me!"

"I believe you, Mourad."

"Because I'm telling you, Father: I did do my rounds. The aisle, the chapels, the ambulatory, the sacristy, the kitchens, the basements, the changing rooms ..."

"I believe you."

"Then why doesn't the rector believe me?"

"I don't know, Mourad, I don't know. I guess the police have given him another story. I guess in their eyes it's the only possible explanation for the tragedy on Sunday night."

"You see, Father, that's the problem. Between a Frenchman and an Arab, it'll always be the Frenchman they'll believe. Automatically, without even thinking."

"What you say applies to the whole country. What did the rector say to you?"

"That once this has all settled down, as he said, there'll be a disciplinary meeting. What does that mean, Father?"

"It means that you'll have to explain yourself, Mourad."

"What's there for me to explain? How can I prove whether or not I did my rounds?"

"Let me tell you something: when the time comes, if you're called by the disciplinary committee, you'll have the right to have someone with you. If you like, that someone can be me."

Mourad looked at him askance. "That's very nice of you, Father. Is that your 'I defend Arabs and thieves, I defend the murderers in Poissy' side? Is that your 'good Christian, good boy' side? Thank you very much, Father, but let me tell you something: this isn't Poissy and I'm neither a murderer nor a thief. With all due respect, you can keep your pity. And If I say I did my job properly, then it's true. And I shouldn't need to have a priest next to me to make people believe it."

He drained his coffee in one gulp and walked away toward the inside of the cathedral, turning up the volume of the radio he wore at his belt, right next to his jangling key chain.

Father Kern got up with difficulty from the chest he was sitting on. He was already feeling pain in his lower limbs. Forgetting about the pay phone and the deputy magistrate for a moment, he went through the external door, down the stone steps and walked in the direction of the rector's residence. He immediately saw him, leaning against the dark wall of his presbytery. Father de Bracy also noticed Father Kern, and started walking toward him. The two priests met at the door of Saint-Étienne.

"Have you come out for air, Monsignor?"

"It's so hot up there in the presbytery. It's unbearable. Remind me which tobacco you smoke, François."

"Peterson, Monsignor. A Virginia-based blend. You don't smoke, do you?"

"No, I don't. I did when I was younger, but that was a long time ago. Were you coming to see me, François?"

"I've just heard that Mourad is going to appear before the disciplinary committee."

"Not anymore. I'm going to leave poor Mourad alone, and the cathedral is finally going to be able to resume its liturgical life."

"How come? What's happening, Monsignor?"

"I've just received a call from the Minister himself. All this regrettable business is over."

"The Minister?"

"The Minister of Justice. Surely you're aware of his special interest in our cathedral. One could say that the suspect has just signed his entire confession."

"'One could say?' What do you mean?"

"The young man committed suicide early this afternoon. A tragedy. Apparently, he jumped from the fourth floor right in the middle of an interrogation. By the time they took him to the Hôtel-Dieu hospital, he was already dead."

Sitting on top of the stone wall, his legs swinging above the water, Gombrowicz watched the Seine flow by. Half an hour earlier, he'd come out of Number 36. He'd crossed the street, heedless of the traffic. Without thinking, driven by a peculiar need to see the waters flow, he'd gone down the paved alley that led to the river. He knew perfectly well that when he went back, he'd have to tell them what he'd seen, what had happened. An hour. They'd given him an hour to calm down and regroup. He searched for words while looking at the flowing Seine. He tried to alter the images in his head into a logical sequence of sentences, but couldn't really manage it.

Words had never been Gombrowicz's strong point. Ever since police academy, perhaps even since high school, he wasn't quite sure, reports, paperwork, and minutes were for him a cross to bear. God only knew how many reports a cop had to write over the course of his career.

Once he was up there, they'd ask him to provide his version of the facts, after they'd heard Landard, after they'd questioned the young deputy. They'd ask him to transform feelings into words. What on earth was he going to tell the Police Inspection Committee people?

I was down in the courtyard of Number 36. I was sitting on the front wing of the Peugeot 308. I was finishing my panini. I was thinking of having a cigarette before going back up.

Just what was he going to tell them?

I had just opened my can of orange Fanta. I leaned my head back to drink and looked up.

What should he tell them? Should he mention the feeling he'd had since yesterday, which had prevented him from sleeping much of the night?

I could see very clearly that the boy was at the end of his tether. I'd already seen it in the car, last night, on the way back, after the search. Landard was driving at breakneck speed and the little lady, sitting next to him in the passenger seat, was staring at the road not saying anything, looking like she'd be on sick leave before the year is out.

Just what should he tell them?

I could see perfectly well that the kid would snap. Already in the car, last night, I felt he was shaking like a leaf. Then, when we took him down to the cells at the Palais for the night, I felt his arm give way. When Landard told him he'd be body searched, he started crying like a baby.

What could they possibly ask him?

Did he eat his cup of instant soup in the cell last night? How should I know? Did they have enough of it to go around? Because they looked rather full last night. Who did he spend the night with? Who else was in his twenty-three-foot cell? I don't really know. What I do know is that he didn't look good in the morning. Obviously, the Palais cells aren't exactly the Ritz. Coffee, yes. Of course he had the right to a coffee. I even bought him one. For once, the machine was working.

What should he tell them? Tell them exactly what he thought?

Let me tell you, there's something in this business that doesn't add up. From the very beginning, something about it has been bothering me.

Should he hush his gut feeling and stick to the facts? To the courtyard at Number 36? To the panini? To the front wing of the Peugeot 308?

I leaned my head back to drink my orange Fanta and I saw him at the window. I saw him go through the window at incredible speed. Like a contortionist coming out of a small box, if you like, with his arms and legs out in front, but in fast-forward.

Should he tell them about that odd feeling? The feeling that time had suddenly stopped during the fall?

Then he fell but slowly, like in slow motion. And in a deathly silence. Like a dead leaf, like a leaf that's too light. Or like an angel. At least to start with. Because the closer he got to the ground, the heavier he seemed. Do you see what I mean? And the fall grew faster. Because when he touched the ground of the courtyard, there was a very dull thud, very strange, very heavy, like a piano crashing down, but without the notes. Do you see what I mean? Just the sound of bones. The sound of bones breaking, but without the notes.

However, what he didn't need to tell them was that when he'd seen the kid dead at his feet, he'd screamed. That was something he remembered extremely clearly: he dropped his can of orange Fanta and started screaming like a man possessed. And the whole of Number 36 was looking out of their windows to see what was happening.

The itching seemed to be coming from deep inside his flesh. It was as though a foreign, living, demented body had penetrated his body and chosen his joints to start eating away at his insides. Scratching was no use. Or else he would do it until he drew blood, until his skin gave and opened up, until his nails could dig through the flesh and claw at cartilage and bones.

The fever had kept him nailed to his bed from as early as eight in the evening. He'd tried to take the old Bayard alarm clock apart once again, but a shooting pain in his wrist made him drop the screwdriver. The attack was so violent, he'd had to give in to it. Without even going to the trouble of undressing, he'd lain down on his mattress, a small, dark silhouette on a white sheet, a marionette made of wretched, dried up wood, lost in the immensity of a bed. On the table, the alarm clock had been left half dismantled, its parts strewn in front of the black and white photo of his brother, while a couple of yards away, Father Kern was trying to forget that he possessed a body.

There was no possible relief. He'd known that since he was a child. Ever since that day when, at the age of five or six, he'd noticed the red splotches appear for the first time on his hands and neck and cried out, "Mommy!" The fever and the redness had returned the following evening, and the day after that. After four days of this pattern, in addition to which he'd then had sharp pains in his hands and wrists, they decided to put a pair of pajamas and his fluffy rabbit in a suitcase, and go to the hospital. He stayed there for three months.

They did everything to him—biopsies, lumbar punctures, blood tests—often fearing the worst, in particular cancer of the lymphatic system—then discarded all their theories one by one and in the end agreed on one final diagnosis. The illness was not deadly. That was the good news. The bad news was that nobody knew where it came from, or how to cure it.

And so the child returned home. The attacks subsided but then came back with a vengeance less than a year later, sending him to the hospital once again. The doctors soon gave up on the huge doses of aspirin and administered equally huge doses of cortisone. The evening pains eventually subsided and they decided, from one attack to the next, as years went by, to make regular use of corticosteroids at every new alarm.

In between one stay in the hospital and another, the child aged rather than grew. The cost of relief and comfort from the arthritic pain was to give up normal growth, normal muscle mass, a normal skeleton, a normal childhood. The others, friends from elementary school, then junior high, then high school, grew, played football, threw parties, kissed the girls sitting next to them in class, and eventually distanced themselves from the pale schoolmate who did not want to grow, and who would disappear from the classroom for weeks on end in order to be treated for nobody knew what exactly at the Necker Hospital.

Through this lasting nightmare that had taken him from childhood to adulthood with more or less the same body, young Kern had had three true friends.

The first was his old Bayard alarm clock, which he'd taken apart and put back together about ten thousand times, every evening hoping to forget about the pain or the itching, trying to understand why fate had somehow decided to put a definitive stop to the passing of time sometime around the age of five or six.

The second was actually the person who'd given him the alarm clock, bought from a secondhand shop with his pocket money, broken, rusted, and in a bad state. His older brother was as blond as he himself was dark, as vigorous as he himself was puny. And yet in all those years, this very different older brother had never, so to speak, let go of his hand during the nights of attacks when young Kern could no longer contain the fire burning inside him.

The third he'd met later in life, at the end of his aborted adolescence, at an age when boys are more interested in what goes on under girls' skirts than in spiritual matters. And as though by another turn of fate, by a strange pendulum effect, it was when young Kern discovered God that his older brother swung into delinquency.

The diminutive priest reached out for the switch above his bed and put out the light. The only hope now, the only thing left to do was to get through the night like a long, dark, silent, frightening tunnel, and wait for morning. At the first rays of the sun, the itching and pain would subside. Daybreak would mark, at least for a few hours, the end of his torture. That, he knew. He believed in it wholeheartedly. It was not a question of faith but of experience of pain.

His thoughts strayed, then focused on the young blond man they'd arrested in the middle of the confessional, and who was now resting in a drawer at the morgue. He opened his eyes and, in the fading daylight, looked again at the photo of his brother. He couldn't help but notice the resemblance. In the blond hair, in the going astray, in the madness, and in death.

Once again, he'd failed. He'd not been able to prevent Thibault's tragic end, which rang like a sinister echo to that of his older brother. He could have banged his head against the wall, screamed with anger against his Lord and God.

Kern let himself drown in pain. It was as though four steel nails had pierced through his ankles and wrists. He, too, was locked in. A life sentence. He was no better than Djibril deep in his prison, but this time the bars were made of suffering, of his family history, of his condition as a man. He would relive again and again the moment when he'd been sentenced to life, and the verdict had to be repeated to him over and over and over again. You lost your brother; you abandoned him in the face of death; and your burning will never be extinguished.

Outside, the August light was deserting this portion of the earth's surface. It must have been about ten o'clock. He closed his eyes again, put his head back on the pillow, and listened to the last city sounds vanish along with the day. Then he thought, "Here we go, I'm entering the tunnel. This time, I have no choice, it's the moment of truth."

They're now walking in single file, ten-yard intervals between them. They've not said a word for nearly two hours, not since the Sikorsky unloaded them in an ocher and beige whirlwind without taking the time to land, suspended three feet above the ground, letting out of its obese flanks the clusters of men in camouflage outfits. The column is now stretching along the hillside like a snake quietly slithering over the dust of the track. Shadows fall. The temperature is dropping by the minute. The sun has hidden behind the mountains. It's like a wave of ink swallowing up the entire area, slowly rising from the bottom of the neighboring valleys. The colleague in front of you is already no more than a form barely distinguishable from the heaps of sand and khaki in the landscape. They will soon have to go down a level and keep walking following the thalweg, at the bot-tom, along the partly dried-up wadi they've been ordered to comb before they reach the village.

Ahead, the sergeant has raised his arm. The column immediately halts, every man's eyes fixed on the one in front of him. The young second lieutenant goes up to his sergeant and pulls a map out of his pocket. Together they assess the location. They speak in a whisper, just a thread of voice that dissolves immediately in the immense setting, like the silly little brook that flows down below in a bed that looks too big for it. After a while, the second lieutenant puts his map back in his pocket and drinks from his flask. He hands it to the sergeant, who refuses with an imperceptible sign of the head. The young lieutenant empties the flask and wipes his mouth with the back of his hand. The sergeant watches him for a moment, the blink of an eye, saying nothing, his eyes expressing a slight reproach that the other man pretends not to notice, then he raises his arm again, indicating the bottom of the valley to the dozen men who are calmly waiting. Still in silence, the column begins its descent. The long human serpent now curls down the slope. A tiny cloud of dust rises in its path now that it has veered off the track. The men take care to keep their distance. They slide more than walk toward the abyss, their leg muscles tensed to the maximum, their eyes and the barrels of their weapons pointing at that unknown area, its outlines blurred and already plunged in darkness. As they progress downward, night seems to be coming up to greet them. The tiny brook has suddenly turned into a black river about to burst its banks. Just a few more yards, ten at most, and they'll all be swallowed up.

THURSDAY

"Look, Father, I had a really bad day yesterday, a really bad night and, in addition, there's a heap of problems waiting for me today. So I can't spare you very much time. You wished to see me? What is this concerning? Unfortunately, we don't have any coffee. Would you care to sit down anyway?"

His limbs still numb after his night's ordeal, Father Kern leaned with both hands on the back of the chair opposite the deputy magistrate's desk, but did not sit down. It was not nine yet but the room was already stiflingly hot, a remainder of the previous day's soaring temperatures. Back to the wall, legs crossed, her hair in a tight bun, Claire Kauffmann was looking at the priest with a seemingly cold, detached expression. She knew it only too well: the calm was just a façade. For the past eight hours, she'd done nothing but turn over in her mind, to the point of obsession, that parenthesis of a few seconds, that brief lack of attention, that very slight inclination to empathy that had allowed the blond angel to free himself from his handcuffs and jump out of the open window. Naturally, she hadn't slept a wink. What had possessed her to inform him in person of the extension of his custody period? What had possessed her to go and make a show to him—him, the little sexual pervert—of her power as a magistrate? Usually, it was the police officers who took care of such formalities and didn't need a deputy to be present. Usually, the public prosecutor's office watched things from a distance. Why did she have to butt in, and open a chink in the armor she'd spent years assembling piece by piece?

"Mademoiselle Kauffmann, I've come to convey to you some important information. I would have much preferred to do it yesterday."

Claire Kauffmann did not blink, motionless on her chair. However, she swallowed with difficulty, and saw that Father Kern had noticed. "What information are you talking about, Father?"

"A witness's testimony. A vagrant. He spoke to me yesterday morning, shortly after opening time."

"Yesterday morning? Why didn't you immediately go to the police?"

"I don't know, madame. Instead of going to the Crime Squad, I chose to come to the Palais de Justice."

The deputy magistrate looked away and stared out the window. "You made a mistake there, Father."

"I know that only too well."

Claire Kauffmann grew a little tense on her chair. "What do you know, exactly?"

"I know, madame, that your principal suspect is dead."

"How long have you known?"

"Since yesterday. Yesterday, late afternoon. The rector of the cathedral told me."

This time, Claire Kauffmann did not try to conceal her annoyance. "I see news travels fast between the Palais de Justice and Notre Dame de Paris."

Father Kern rubbed it in. "I know that he killed himself

in the middle of the day by jumping out of the window of the police office where he was being questioned."

"In that case, Father, you also know that it's now too late, and that the testimony of your vagrant, whatever it contains, is no longer of any use to us."

"Excuse me?"

"The case has been shelved."

"Shelved? By whom?"

"By the public prosecutor's office. They decided that there was no more reason for any follow-up."

"The public prosecutor's office? Who, exactly? You?"

"I don't have to answer that."

"Did you receive the order from above?"

"I don't have to answer your questions, Father."

"Who ordered you to shelve it?"

"I don't have to answer your questions! Do I need to remind you that it's the prosecution's prerogative? The public prosecutor has decided that the suspect's suicide was tantamount to a confession. Case closed. Neither you nor I can do anything about it."

"The public prosecutor? Since when is fear the equivalent of a confession? Since when are bewilderment and mental illness equivalent to a confession? Since when is death the equivalent of a confession? Did you even listen to that boy? Did you even talk to him?"

"Father, we're not in a confessional but at the Palais de Justice. Here we deal with criminal matters. We don't ask ourselves if a decision is moral but whether it's legal. The law. That's our gospel."

"Can't you make an exception?"

"I'm sorry, but we're not here to hand out pardons by the shovelful."

"Mademoiselle Kauffmann, I've come to bring you positive proof—positive, do you hear?—that the boy who died yesterday was innocent."

"Innocent? What's all this about?"

"The night of the murder, at about ten o'clock, when it was already dark, a young woman dressed in white went into the cathedral gardens. In order to do that, she opened the gate in Rue du Cloître, a gate secured with a padlock the combination to which is known only to cathedral staff. She walked through the darkness, and climbed the few steps that lead to a little door at the back of the building. That door immediately opened. Apparently, somebody was waiting for her. The young woman walked into the cathedral. She came back out only the following morning, on your medical examiner's stretcher, on her way to the morgue. Now, a man saw the scene at night which I've just described. His name is Krzysztof, he's a down-and-out Polish man who sleeps on Square Jean-XXIII every night, right next door to the cathedral. From his makeshift bed he has an unrestricted view of the cathedral gardens and apse. Madame, you, who at this point are convinced you have your culprit—would you be kind enough to answer just these few questions of a simple parish priest, an insignificant priest who's trying to see clearly in the darkness: Why did the victim enter through the back of the cathedral? What mysterious meeting was she going to? How did she know the combination of the padlock in Rue du Cloître? And who opened the door to let her in?" Mademoiselle Kauffmann, it's up to you now, and I'm listening."

She held out five, perhaps ten seconds without stirring, without saying anything, almost without breathing. Then, suddenly, she started to cry, and her tears came falling down on the knees she kept obstinately together. Briefly disconcerted, Father Kern finally let go of the chair back he'd been digging his fingers into, leaving a mark on the orange plastic. He walked around the desk, took a handkerchief out of his pocket, and held it out to the young magistrate. She swiveled sideways on her chair, blew her nose, and finally managed to control her sobs.

"Your handkerchief smells of pipe tobacco."

"That's possible. I'm sorry about that."

"No, on the contrary, it reminds me of my father. He, too, smoked a pipe. His gown was always steeped in the smell of tobacco."

"His gown?"

"He was a lawyer."

Father Kern decided to sit opposite the young woman. "I owe you an apology. I'm afraid I got up on my high horse earlier. You must have been deeply affected by this tragic death."

"He jumped right before my eyes. I saw him vanish through the window. Immediately afterward, somebody started screaming down in the courtyard."

"Are you going to get into trouble now?"

She sniffed, and blew her nose again. "The public prosecutor has asked for a preliminary inquest to be opened. Later this morning, I have to appear before the PIC and the LIC."

"That's a lot of initials for just one person to come up against."

"It's the Police Inspection Committee and the Legal Inspection Committee. Afterwards, they'll decide whether or not to start disciplinary procedure."

"But you weren't on your own in that office. There must also have been a police officer? Wasn't the young man his responsibility?"

"There was Landard, of course, but you know ... Landard is Landard. I think it was he who reported me."

"Why would he implicate you?"

"Because it's my fault, you see. I insisted that the window be opened. I insisted that his handcuffs be removed. It all went wrong."

"You couldn't have foreseen that he'd jump."

"It's all gone wrong. Since the beginning. I realize that now. From the moment I saw that girl's body. I've taken this whole case too much to heart. I contributed to the turning of this machine that mangled him in less than two days. I also wanted him to confess. I was sure that there was a pervert under that angelic expression. It was too good to be true. A regular madman. The ideal culprit. That's what he was. For the police, for the media, for the public prosecutor's office. The ideal culprit. And he still is. His death changes nothing." She started to laugh and, after her bout of tears, the laugh made her look like a child again. "Good God. I've been on the side of the police for so long. Me, the little thirty-year-old magistrate who goes off on a crusade against ogres, monsters, and sexual predators. It's absurd. Absurd and an illusion. It fixes nothing. Never. What's done is done."

Kern waited. His experience as a confessor had taught him to be patient and silent when faced with a door that was slowly opening by itself, after being locked for a long time.

"You're going to think I seek absolution. Against all expectation, the little public prosecutor turns to religion. What should be done, then? Give me instructions, Father. What should be done? Beat one's chest and say, 'I confess to God almighty?'"

Silence fell over them. The image of a bird banging against the bars of its cage briefly flashed before the priest's eyes. "Tell me, Claire. When did it happen? Was it a long time ago?"

The young woman's eyes froze. At first, Kern thought that they were lost in the void but then immediately realized that they were looking to the past.

"The summer when I was sixteen. One evening, on the beach."

"Have you ever talked about it to anyone?"

"The sound of waves has made me want to vomit ever since. I tell people I get seasick. It's my excuse for never going to the shore. No, Father, never. I've never told anyone about it."

She brushed an invisible speck of dust from the fold in her skirt.

"It's not too late, Claire."

"How would you know?"

"We all carry our burden. That part of us that's dead forever, and that we have to drag around wherever we go. Christ also carried his cross a very long way. He carried it to the end of his suffering. Three days later he was resurrected and, with him, the hope of a new life. The cross isn't the goal but the baggage, Claire. Sooner or later one must resolve to put it down."

Once again, the magistrate's eyes grew misty. She chose to look away as Kern stood up.

"You know where to find me if you need me, don't you? I'm here if you want to talk. Don't hesitate."

"Thank you, Father. But it won't bring our innocent man back from the dead, you know."

She looked much older now, and her childhood seemed to have vanished forever. She took a pencil and a notepad. "So, your Polish vagrant—where can one find him?"

Kern hesitated for a brief moment. "It's of no importance. The case is shelved anyway, you said so yourself. Only a miracle could reopen the investigation and there will be no miracle, I think I can safely assure you of that."

"What makes you suddenly so certain? If you have an important piece of information in your possession, it could contribute to reopening the case."

"Who insisted that the case be shelved? The Paris prosecutor?"

"Yes. He called me very early this morning. I was still at home."

"And the prosecutor probably received the same phone call from the Ministry."

"I don't understand. What has the Ministry got to do with this?"

"Mademoiselle Kauffmann, do you know who the Knights of the Holy Sepulcher of Jerusalem are?"

"I came across that name in the file."

"They don't just carry the statue of the Virgin Mary once a year on the day of the Assumption, you know. It's an order that dates back to the medieval Crusaders. Naturally, they no longer defend a fortress with a sword. Their aim is to support the Christian community in the Holy Land through charitable deeds. And also to evangelize modern Western society. Their network extends over thirty or so countries, including France."

"So?"

"Did you know the capitular chapel of the Order of the Holy Sepulcher is situated at Notre Dame de Paris? It would have taken just a phone call to restore long-term calm over the cathedral. There's only about five hundred yards between Notre Dame and the Palais de Justice, but the quickest way from one to the other is sometimes across the Place Vendôme."

"Are you saying that your knights have their own entrance to the Ministry of Justice?"

"The Minister himself is one of them. That's why I am now sure that your investigation is well and truly buried."

Propped up against her chair, Claire Kauffmann had now completely recovered her calm. Only her eyes seemed strangely mobile, betraying the train of thought unraveling in her mind. Kern made a gesture suggesting he was about to hold out his hand to the young woman, then changed his mind. "The law has found its culprit, Mademoiselle Kauffmann, that's the truth. Apparently, the Church is also satisfied. A lunatic, a madman who will soon be forgotten. As for the victim's parents, they'll be asked to bury their daughter quietly, somewhere out of the way, that is, unless the poor child has already been buried."

"No, not yet. The burial is tomorrow at three p.m. at the Montmartre cemetery."

"They will seal her grave with official cement and the parents will have to accept that. 'Your daughter was murdered by a madman, end of story, move along ladies and gentlemen, no point in making an official complaint.' Who would want to reopen an investigation everyone considers to have come full circle? Who?"

Claire Kauffmann crossed her legs. She was breathing a little more quickly. She was looking at Father Kern with an odd intensity. "I have a run in my pantyhose."

The priest couldn't help sliding a glance down the young magistrate's legs. "Excuse me?"

"I've snagged my pantyhose. I need to go out and change them."

And mechanically, blushing, she grabbed a paper clip from her desk, unfurled it, and passed the tip over her knee. The sheer mesh that concealed her skin immediately burst open and the run extended three or four inches up her pale thigh. The young woman stood up and walked past Father Kern, who was speechless. She went to the door, grabbed the handle, and, without turning around, said, in a flat, almost inaudible, slightly trembling voice, "The Notre Dame case file is in my desk. The key's in the lock. The search and interrogation reports, the postmortem results, the medical examiner's report—it's all there. My colleague's in the clerk's office, so won't be back for at least half an hour. I'll be away for ten minutes exactly. That's how long I'm giving you. When I return, I'd like to see the file back the way it was, where you found it. You may use the photocopier, if you wish. You just have to press the green button to get it out of sleep mode. Goodbye, Father."

She half-opened the door and was gone in a flash. He heard her footsteps fading down the corridor.

How long did he stay there, his arms dangling, standing before the desk heaped with files, in that tiny room that smelled of paperwork and dust? How long before he realized just what the magistrate had whispered to him? Time seemed to have stopped, and the blood in his veins froze. In the distance, he heard the bells of Notre Dame ring for the nine a.m. Mass, and he finally came out of his torpor. Then, slowly, his heart beating like that of a child afraid to be punished by his parents, he walked around the deputy magistrate's desk and unlocked the drawer.

Kern drank his coffee in one gulp. He'd let it cool down for several long minutes without saying anything, making the liquid spin at the bottom of the glass, as a reflection of the dark thoughts he was prey to, looking worried, absorbed, stalling for time because his indecision was so great it was preventing him from doing what he'd come to do. Opposite him, sitting on the stool that looked too fragile to bear his weight, leaning his elbows on his knees, holding the jar of Nescafé in his paws, Djibril was watching the diminutive priest with his piercing eyes. "You look like a guy who's come to confess but doesn't know where to begin, François."

The priest put the glass down at the foot of the bed he was sitting on. He plunged his hand into the inside pocket of his jacket and pulled out a stack of photocopies folded three times. Without a word, he held it out to Djibril. The prisoner put down the jar of instant coffee and began to look through the document, which had been stapled at one of the corners.

"Are these the committing magistrate's records?"

"No, those of the public prosecutor's office. Now that the case is closed, they won't be appointing a judge."

"Much simpler, this way. Those little judges are too independent. They could go and stick their noses somewhere it stinks, right?"

"I don't know. What do you think of the file?"

"At first glance, it doesn't look very thick."

"They already got their culprit, so why go look elsewhere?"

"How did you get it?"

"The young magistrate in charge of the case let me see it."

"She's taking a big risk."

"I know. She's breaking the confidentiality of the investigation."

"From what you're telling me, that's not her only problem. She's also got the General Investigators hot on her heels, right?"

"What do you think of the file? You're quite right, I don't know where to begin. I glanced at it on the train. There's nothing interesting in the interrogation transcripts. As for the search, how can I put it? Well, it just confirms that the kid wasn't comfortable with his sexuality."

A wide smile spread across the prisoner's face. He was paying particular attention to one of the pages in the file. With his thumbnail, he opened the staple that kept the sheets together. Father Kern briefly pictured a bulldozer gently tearing a nail out of a plank.

"I really like this one. Do you mind? In any case, it'll look better here than at your place. Just a question of consistency. After all, I'm the murderer here."

Keeping his naughty boy expression, he stuck one of the

drawings seized from young Thibault's home to the wall. "If you don't mind, I'll keep the others for my friends. All right?"

Kern knew Djibril too well to let himself be rattled by his blasphemous provocations. He nodded without saying anything. The prisoner looked a little longer at the photocopy on his wall, which was insignificant in the midst of photos taken from porn magazines, then sat back down and resumed looking through the rest of the stack. Kern picked up where the prisoner had interrupted him. "The crime scene investigations have yielded nothing, or not much. Too many people involved, too many marks. It was to be expected. We're talking about the most visited monument in France here. As for the postmortem report, they found young Thibault's DNA on the victim. Among others. Once again, she spent the day in all the bustle, in the middle of a crowd. Does what Thibault left on her correspond to the first attack or to the murder? Nobody can tell. The poor girl definitely died of strangling but the marks on her throat say no more. One assumes the murderer wore gloves, and that the body was moved after death. I don't know. All the pieces of information cancel one another out. Where to go from here? Where to look? After all, I'm just a priest, I know nothing about being a policeman."

Djibril was reading. He didn't even bother to look up from the file. "If you were working for the cops, François, you wouldn't have come to see me and I wouldn't have opened my door to you. So to speak, of course. Not that I get to decide who opens my door."

"Of course, there's that strange thing of the wax in her vagina, which suggests the theory of a madman, a lunatic, but—"

"You must search around the girl."

"Excuse me?"

"You must search around your dead girl. In this file of yours, there's barely enough information about her to fill a postage stamp."

"She was a student without any background."

"The cops totally botched their investigation. From what I'm reading here, they just paid a superficial visit to the girl's room at her parents' apartment and stopped there." He handed the stack of papers back to Kern and concluded, with a smile, "In other words, a bad job—the kind they say we Arabs do."

Kern put the file back in his jacket pocket and looked at his watch. "I've only just got time to get there."

"Where?"

"Her funeral. It's in Montmartre at three."

The two men stood up and shook hands.

"Leaving already?"

"Thanks for your invaluable help, Djibril."

"I'll have my secretary send you an invoice. Keep me posted, will you? It's important to me."

"You're hooked now, aren't you? The priest and the prisoner. We make quite a pair of investigators."

Djibril smiled. Kern felt him distance himself, escape through his restricted cell to a time and space where he could never follow. The priest knew full well that, despite the doors, the visiting rooms, the hours devoted to his activity as chaplain every week, the boundary between the outside and the inside of the prison was impassable. With every extra minute of being locked up, the walls in this purgatory of iron and concrete grew thicker. Djibril was gradually slipping away from the world, and nobody and nothing could ever bring him back among the living.

Kern squeezed the prisoner's icy hand a little tighter. "What you've just done for me ... I don't know. Your advice, this conversation. Isn't that proof of good behavior? Perhaps I could mention it to the sentencing judge, so he relaxes—"

Djibril let go of the priest's hand. "Don't bother, priest. For him I'm just a murderer—period. And he's right. There's no redemption possible here. Besides, all we did was talk about the weather, you know that perfectly well. The photocopy you've just let me read doesn't officially exist."

"That's true. You're right. I'm sorry I can't help you more."

"You're wrong, François. I've already started to be rewarded. As of today, I'm going to think about something else. Put my imagination to work, think about your case while I clean my teeth at night. You know, in Poissy this kind of occupation is priceless. Here, my life revolves around this kettle and my jar of coffee."

"You know that's not true."

"You know it is, priest."

The priest walked around the three-foot-high wall that separated the bed from the toilet bowl, and reached the cell door in a couple of strides.

"Get ready for quite a ride, François. Don't be surprised if you meet a few ghosts on the way."

"I meet ghosts during my sleepless nights, Djibril. Every night, I also take a trip around purgatory. And it hasn't killed me yet."

Kern turned the handle. The abrupt click of the mechanism made the prisoner take a step back.

"This time, you could well go as far as hell, priest. Your nice prayers will be of no use to you there. In fact, perhaps you'd better remove the cross from your lapel. Where you're going, it will only make it easier to spot you, trust me."

The door opened, revealing in the corridor a guard's uniform. Father Kern looked at the prisoner one more time, then disappeared down the corridor lit with pale fluorescent lights.

Behind him, the reinforced door closed again with a cavernous thud.

Luna Hamache had only just been buried when Father Kern arrived at Section 14 of the Montmartre Cemetery. Heavily, almost in slow motion, doubly knocked out by grief as well as the heat, a group of thirty or so people milled around the grave at a respectful distance from a couple who remained rooted right on the edge of the pit, perfectly still, as though cut in stone. Both in their fifties, the dead woman's parents presented faces without tears, as though they hadn't yet comprehended the exact reason for their being in this cemetery, as though the plain, bare coffin that was now resting at the bottom of a grave had not belonged to their daughter but to somebody else, a stranger whose funeral they were attending by chance. The father, especially, seemed alienated from himself. His gaze had trouble lingering on the bottom of the pit and would regularly stray toward the entrance to the cemetery, as though Luna would appear there at any minute, in the full bloom of her youth, and prove the gravediggers and death wrong.

A young woman went up the line, handing out a white rose to each person, and Kern noticed that almost the entire group was made up of young people dressed in white. With a solemnity at odds with their age—they were all in their twenties—Luna's fellow students paraded before the grave, which was still wide open, and threw their flowers on the lid of the coffin, suppressing a sob or muttering a few words that were immediately absorbed by the noise of the surrounding traffic. While they paraded like this, Kern caught the eye of a man who was standing apart, one shoulder against a tree, his arms crossed. The priest made a sign to Lieutenant Gombrowicz, to which the latter responded with a nod.

Finally, two gravediggers from the Paris municipality came to say a few words to the dead woman's parents. Her mother nodded twice, mechanically, then gave a circular look of thanks to those who were standing around the grave. The group broke up with difficulty, as though everyone had lead soles on their shoes, while the cemetery employees began work without delay on closing the grave. Luna's parents watched them a little while longer, then the mother took her husband by the arm. They walked a few steps down the alley, like two old people unsteadily supporting each other, suddenly alone in the world and deprived of their main reason for remaining standing. On their way, they saw a little man with a thin hatchet face and a cross on his lapel. He went up to them and shook their hands warmly.

"I'm Father Kern. I'm the one who found your daughter's body in Notre Dame on Monday morning."

Luna Hamache's mother looked at him for a moment without saying anything, while the father kept his eyes fixed on the entrance to the cemetery. She finally spoke, but her hesitant voice revealed her distress before the representative of the very place where her daughter had died.

"Thank you for coming, Father. We received a note from your rector this morning."

"Monsignor de Bracy, yes."

"He wrote that he'd had a prayer said. Of course, it was nice to receive the letter, but ..."

"But it doesn't explain anything. Does it?"

"Did you know my daughter? Had you already seen her in Notre Dame?"

Her eyes filled with pleading and Kern found himself stammering one of the most minimalistic replies he could have. "No,

I'm sorry, Madame Hamache, I didn't know Luna. We've all prayed for her."

"I don't understand. Nobody is explaining anything to us. The murderer's suicide has left us totally distraught. The authorities seem to have forgotten us already. They seem to have moved on already. It's like a wall without a door, we don't know where to knock to find out more about the attack that ... As for Luna going to the Assumption ceremony, she never mentioned she had an interest in the Catholic faith. As you can see, we're what they call nowadays a mixed couple. We've always allowed our daughter the freedom to choose whichever religion she thought best. Until now it's a matter she'd never talked to us about. We're trying to understand but nobody seems able to tell us anything, not your rector and not you, Father. We bury our daughter and, with her, something of an unresolved mystery."

Kern felt a sense of unease grow in him. He should try and soothe the pain of these two parents, and the cross he wore on his lapel seemed to have largely contributed to the spontaneous outpouring of Luna's mother, yet he was aware of the real reason for his being at the cemetery. His true motivations were those of an investigator, and he was bringing with him more questions about Luna than answers to her mother's queries.

"Your daughter was twenty-one, Madame Hamache. An age of much questioning, and also an age where one searches for some form of independence. Perhaps she didn't speak to you at all about it. Perhaps she had a sort of secret garden."

"We did feel she was somewhat distancing herself in the past few months. Yes, a desire for independence we couldn't satisfy."

"What do you mean?"

"What I mean, Father, is that we're not rolling in money. At the beginning of the academic year, Luna wanted to move out and get a little apartment nearby, with a female friend from the university. She'd sometimes spend the night away from home. More and more often, in fact. But we couldn't afford to help her with rent. My husband studied in Algeria, you see. His qualifications have never been recognized in France. Our marriage couldn't change anything. For twenty years, he worked doing odd jobs at an IT firm. He did small repairs, helped out around the office, took care of deliveries. Three years ago, they fired him. He can't find another job at his age. We live on my salary as a home care worker, so we can't give our daughter a good start in life. Well, anyway, she doesn't need it now."

Madame Hamache's chin began to quiver, and she clenched her jaw. Kern waited. His questions were turning into an interrogation, but conducted with the gentleness of a confessor.

"Do you know who she wanted to share the apartment with?"

"Yes, of course, with Nadia. Her best friend. They study—studied—at the university together."

"Was Nadia here today?"

"She was the one who distributed the roses, earlier. You must have seen her. She's also the one who asked Luna's friends to wear white. Nice girl, Nadia. She wanted to say goodbye to her in her own way. She's been deeply affected by my daughter's death. She was the one who called us on Tuesday morning to say there was the picture in *Le Parisien*, and an appeal for witnesses."

"I thought it was Monsieur Hamache who'd read it in the paper."

"No, it was Nadia. After she called, my husband went downstairs to check the paper in the café. Afterwards, we called the police."

Hearing his name mentioned, Luna's father had emerged from his torpor. He turned to look at the priest, as though noticing him for the first time, and Kern immediately felt the piercing, distraught look that seemed to ask him precisely why he was at the cemetery. Kern stammered a few phrases of comfort. The words came out of his mouth like the lines of a bad actor, as a kind of annoying reflex, and he mentally blamed himself for these fake-sounding platitudes. He said goodbye and walked away along the alley by the grave. After a few steps, he turned to Luna's parents again.

"Madame Hamache, what was your daughter studying?"

And, for the first time, the dead young woman's father unclenched his teeth. "History, monsieur. Luna was doing a degree in history. She was going to be a teacher."

Paris was once again in the grip of a stifling heat wave and the air was heavier than ever. Pollution made it even harder to breathe. Kern left the cemetery by Avenue Rachel. Lieutenant Gombrowicz seemed to have discreetly vanished at the end of the ceremony. Outside the Irish pub on the corner of Boulevard de Clichy, the group of students dressed in white was slowly breaking up with a great deal of hugging. Their immaculate clothes now looked out of place, naive, almost comical, far too much at odds with the urban chaos, the noise of car engines, the smell of gas, and the volley of abuse hurled by the drivers. The priest hesitated. Should he approach the young people? Or wait for their expressions of affection to come to an end? Should he introduce himself with his true identity? Try and obtain information about their friend who was now lying at the bottom of a grave, and to whom they'd come to say a final goodbye? He put his hand in his pocket, pulled out his tobacco pouch, and, as he did whenever he struggled to make up his mind, began to fill his pipe, trying to focus on this harmless activity instead of the stream of conflicting thoughts invading his mind. At the exact moment he was wedging the ebonite tube between his teeth, the young woman who'd handed a white rose to each of her friends left the group. She crossed Boulevard de Clichy, her heels making a clicking sound, and everything became crystal clear. The entire city became concentrated in that pale form that was now walking down the median strip toward Place Blanche. He took the time to light his pipe, drew a few fragrant puffs, then began trailing after Nadia, about twenty yards behind her.

It was a kind of drunkenness, a return to childhood, to the adolescence he'd never experienced: he was playing at following a woman, playing at being a detective in the heat of the city, on this packed boulevard that on either side of the median strip formed a kind of multicolored conveyer belt made of automobile steel, rearview mirrors, and glass windows. Kern smoked his pipe and walked casually, totally absorbed by the strange enjoyment this tailing gave him. An entire battalion of gendarmes in uniform could have followed him in turn, and he wouldn't have noticed.

Nadia left the boulevard when she reached the square, and took Rue Blanche. The priest thought this was a good time to approach her, and picked up the pace. He was just two or three yards away from her when the young woman stopped outside the door of a building adjoining a café. She made a friendly gesture at the waiter serving outside, then reached out for the security keypad with her hand. Taken aback by this sudden stop, Father Kern overtook the young woman without daring to speak to her, just seeing the long, slender fingers skipping on the keypad. He didn't have the presence of mind to memorize the code and was annoyed with himself because of that. The lock clicked abruptly. Nadia pushed the door and disappeared inside.

As a last resort, he sat at a sidewalk table outside the café, choosing a spot from where he could see the door. The waiter, an outsized beanpole with a balding head and cheeks decorated with thick sideburns, immediately approached. He wiped the table with a sponge. Kern ordered a draft beer and put his pipe down on the marble surface, which was still wet. Many years earlier, when he was about sixteen or seventeen, he'd gotten blind drunk with his older brother, on a particularly bad evening when his joints were just too painful. The experiment had not been particularly conclusive, so Kern had decided to swallow his cortisone tablets as the only possible stopgap to his pain.

An old woman with a shopping bag slowly approached, obviously suffering from the heat. She stopped outside the nearby door and, in turn, keyed in the combination that would give access to the relative coolness of her home. Her memory and her hands, less agile than those of the young woman who'd entered earlier, made her press heavily on the keys, giving the priest enough time to memorize the code. Kern drained his glass, paid, and went to the door. However, before letting his increasingly numb fingers run over the keypad, he took care to unclasp the small metal cross on his lapel and slipped it into his wallet. He pushed the door and entered a brownish corridor partly taken up by a block of dilapidated mailboxes. He perused the labels without finding any Nadias, and went past the staircase, to a door leading onto a small courtyard. At this time in the afternoon, the light had already largely abandoned it, so the place looked like a well. Bicycles, a stroller, and children's scooters had been put there hastily. To the left, a door indicated the entrance to a small first-floor apartment, probably a studio. Kern was about to turn back when the door opened wide. Nadia was standing in the doorway, arms crossed, one shoulder against the frame. She'd changed her clothes, and was now wearing a colorful summer dress.

"Are you looking for me?"

"Excuse me?"

"You were at the cemetery earlier on. I saw you talking to Luna's parents. Are you looking for me now?"

"You're Nadia, aren't you?"

"Did you just follow me all the way here?"

"Followed you? No, Luna's mother told me where to find you."

"You know Luna's mother?"

"Yes, of course."

"And what does Luna's mother do for a living?"

"She's a home care worker. Why do you ask?"

"Just checking."

"Good Lord—checking what?"

"You're one of Luna's mother's patients, aren't you?"

"That's right. She's helping me with my physical therapy. Over time we've become friendly. She often talked about Luna. As you can see, I have health problems, problems with my joints. What about you? Were you a friend of Luna's?"

"From the university, yes. Are you a cop?"

"A cop? Not at all. You think I've got the build for it?"

The girl gave him a slight smile. "Then what is it you want?"

"It's hard to say. I'd like to talk about Luna. I didn't really know her but her mother said you were her best friend."

She suddenly disappeared inside, allowing Kern the time to glimpse a few insignificant details at the back: the white tiles of a bathroom, a pink shower curtain with mauve hearts, a bathtub equipped with old-fashioned faucets. Nadia reappeared as quickly as she'd gone, holding a cell phone, the strap of a Louis Vuitton bag wedged in the crook of her arm. She locked the door and stuffed the keys into her bag. "I'm sorry, I have an urgent appointment and I'm running late. And something else:

I've only just left the cemetery, Luna is six feet under. I really don't feel like talking about her right now."

"Yes, of course. I understand. Another time, maybe."

"That's right."

She walked away, leaving behind a heady, sugary scent that seemed to be coming from her hair or the hollow of her neck. Left alone in the middle of bicycles and scooters, in this overheated courtyard, with the fever slowly spreading through his body, and starting to doubt his investigative abilities, Father Kern wondered how many lies he'd just had to tell in less than a minute in order just to get a glimpse of a vague, fleeting bit of bath overhung with a shower curtain.

He walked at random, going back up the street he'd come down earlier. When he reached the boulevard, he paused outside a shop window and began to fill his pipe. He did so with the utmost care, isolating himself from the surrounding noise, focusing his attention on the pinches of tobacco he was pushing one after the other deep into the chamber with a slightly trembling finger. It was only after drawing a few puffs that he noticed he'd stopped outside one of the many sex shops lining the sidewalk. Leaning forward, he examined with a curiosity that had nothing fake about it the various pieces of red and black vinyl underwear, the high-heeled boots and pumps, the nighties with strategic transparency, and the satin nurse's uniforms, while above him, the swirls of Virginia-scented smoke assumed the purple color of the three neon letters that formed the word SEX. He suddenly straightened up and looked around, animated by an urgency that seemed to have unexpectedly come over him. He walked over to Rue Blanche once again, passing Nadia's building without even glancing at it, then, a couple of dozen yards farther on, disappeared into a shop above which there was a luminous @ sign. Father Kern practically assaulted the counter behind which, slumped on his stool, wedged between a fan and a photocopier, sat an Asian man with dark rings under his eyes.

"I'd like a computer. I need to use the Internet."

"You can't smoke in here, boss."

Kern went back out to empty his pipe on the sidewalk, then repeated his request. The other man looked at him with a gloomy expression.

"It's one euro for fifteen minutes. Three euros for an hour."

Kern took out his wallet and put a ten-euro bill flat on the counter. "I need at least two hours. And give me a spot out of the way, please."

As it happened, it took him less than forty minutes to find what he was looking for. Father Kern was savvy with the basic functions of the Internet thanks to Mourad, the cathedral guard who, the previous summer, had agreed to give him a few IT lessons after closing time in the evening. Consequently, the priest had been able to discover countless websites dedicated to collectors of old alarm clocks. At one point, he'd even considered buying a computer, but had never been able to drum up the courage to venture into a store, despite Mourad's offer to go with him.

"I need to make a phone call."

"Have you finished with the machine, boss?"

"Yes, I've finished."

"You booked two hours."

"Yes, I know."

"You've got over an hour left."

"I won't be needing it. What I do need, however, is to make a call."

"Can I give your computer to somebody else?"

"Yes."

"You'll lose your hour."

"Never mind that. I'd like to make a phone call now."

The man on the stool held out his arms toward a row of numbered glass doors with wooden frames. "You've got a choice. Pick whichever you like. Where are you calling?"

"What do you mean where?"

"Which country, boss? Morocco? Tunisia? Algeria?"

"An orange Fanta. And the check."

Gombrowicz had sat at a table from which he could see the end of the street. The waiter brought his drink. "Wouldn't you like to sit outside?"

"I'm comfortable indoors."

"Are you sure? In this heat, you'd be better off at a table outside if you want to see what's going on there."

The police officer gave the waiter an intense look. Then, without saying a word, he turned once again and fixed his eyes on the spot he was staring at outside. The young man, whose cheeks were covered by thick sideburns, walked away with a deep sigh which lasted as far as the counter.

Gombrowicz remained there for an easy half an hour, sitting alone indoors, while customers went to and from the tables on the sidewalk in the vague, diesel-smelling draft caused by the passing buses. He finally got up, after leaving the money for the check in the small plastic dish abandoned next to his glass. He remained in the doorway for a moment, looking down the street, taking the time to light a cigarette before being turned out by the waiter with sideburns, whose comings and goings between the sidewalk and the interior were incessant. He left the café running, neglecting the traditional, automatic "Thanks, bye," as though seized by a sudden urgency to stretch his legs. He crossed the street after letting a bus with a German license plate drive past, and hurtled down the sidewalk across the road, to a shop he dashed into like the wind.

"The guy in the light-colored suit who just left, what was he up to?"

"You can't smoke here, boss."

Gombrowicz took out his police ID from the fanny pack he wore across the shoulder. "I asked you a question, Bruce Lee."

"He bought six dozen spring rolls."

"Don't fuck with me."

"He used the Internet, boss. What else?"

"Is that all?"

"Then he made a call."

"Where to? Do you know?"

"No idea."

"Which computer did he use?"

"The one down there."

The police officer sat at the station and put his hand on the mouse. He clicked on the search history of the session that still hadn't expired. Once he'd scrolled through everything, from the first to the last page viewed by the previous user, he sat back in his chair, lit a cigarette, and stared up at the ceiling.

"Please, boss, you can't smoke in here."

"Old pervert."

"What did you say, boss?"

"I said: disgusting asshole."

And while Gombrowicz was diving back into the stifling heat of Rue Blanche, the Asian man got up, seemingly against his will, from his stool. He went to the computer the police officer had just left. His vacant eyes suddenly lit up when he read the screen:

"North African student, 22, affectionate and sensual, entertains mature and polite men for relaxation and intimacy in Paris

18th. Dark hair—hazel eyes—5 ft 4, 120 lb—natural 34C. 7 p.m. to midnight. Relaxing massage. Manual or oral finish. Affectionate or severe. Four-hand massage possible with a sympathetic friend."

And below the cell phone number, there was an amateur photo taken with a flash, showing a dark-haired young woman with a blurred face posing naked in her bathtub, lifting her heavy breasts with her hands while the curve of her waist, her buttocks, and her sex disappeared behind a pink shower curtain with mauve hearts.

A police officer from the Police Inspection Committee and a female magistrate from the Legal Inspection Committee at 36 Quai des Orfèvres took her testimony during the lunch hour, in a small room that was sometimes used as an interrogation room for criminals caught in the act. They'd fired their volley of questions at her, constantly coming back, like waves, to that moment when everything had gone haywire, when she'd decided to open the window and remove the young prisoner's handcuffs. And Claire Kauffmann had thought, *"How many times are they going to ask me the same question? They keep coming back to it. Each time, they change one or two words in the way they phrase it, but it's always the same question. Are there really so many different ways to report an act that took two or three seconds? Are there so many different angles to view the situation from? Isn't the truth just the truth?"* And the young magistrate would reiterate her explanations over and over again, each time also altering two or three words in her statement.

She'd broken off right in the middle of a sentence, suddenly remembering her morning conversation with Father Kern, wondering if her command that Landard should untie Thibault, a command that had turned out to have such dire consequences, had been dictated by a legal or a moral decision on her part. And the policeman sitting opposite her, who, from the moment the interrogation began, had kept moving his cup of coffee from one side of the table to the other, had rushed into that moment of hesitation. "Basically, you're wondering if you weren't too humane toward the suspect, aren't you?" And since Claire Kauffmann hadn't replied on the spot, he'd insisted, "You're wondering if this brief moment of weakness or—how shall I put it?—of compassion, was the cause of his death, right?"

She came out of the interrogation session feeling completely drained, incapable of forming any thought, however basic, and able only to ask herself if she'd made the right decision in specializing in criminal law. They'd sent her back to her job, to her role as a Sisyphus in pencil skirt and tight hair bun. She didn't yet know if she'd be disciplined. For the investigators, it was a matter of establishing whether young Thibault should have been questioned in a hospital environment rather than in the Crime Squad offices. In other words, the investigation was turning away from her, clinging to technical questions, to procedure, leaving her to face her own questions alone.

She looked at her watch and realized she wouldn't have time for lunch before her next hearing at two o'clock. So she briefly went back up to her office to pick up the file of the tile installer who'd struck his wife with a hammer. On her way, she checked that Father Kern had put the Notre Dame file back in her drawer. She drank a glass of water. Then she appeared in the hearing chamber as though in a foreign country.

The case was settled in the presence of the tile installer's wife, who'd just been released from the hospital. Claire asked for a prison sentence without parole, with special surveillance. She acted like a robot, speaking in the staccato phrases people at the Palais were beginning to be familiar with, without ever lifting her nose from her paperwork.

Finally, after the hearing, she ended up in the huge waiting hall of the Palais de Justice, disorientated and nauseous, stomach empty, with a splitting headache, her heavy files wedged in the crook of her arm. She drowned in the hubbub of the crowd made up of visitors, magistrates, lawyers, and gendarmes. The clicking of her heels on the marble floor sounded distant, reaching her ears only through the echo they produced in the immensity of the place, and which blended in with other surrounding sounds. It was suddenly as though her footsteps no longer belonged to her, as though they were somewhat alien to her. And, all of a sudden, she felt like screaming. And the scream she felt rising from the depths of her bowels reminded her of another scream, the only one she'd ever really let out in all her life.

It was in the high school cafeteria, the year of her Baccalauréat, the year she turned seventeen. A boy in her class had sat next to her at the table, and was talking to her too loudly and too close. Too close, especially. And while he was yelling in her ear to make himself heard above the noise of eight hundred other students in the process of devouring their *steak-frites*, she started to scream. A very shrill scream that seemed neverending, a scream that rose in the air of the cafeteria above everybody else, a scream that had immediately silenced an entire school. A supervisor took her to see the principal, a little man with a mustache, who used to watch the world and his pupils while hiding behind thick glasses, and before whom she'd remained silent, unable to explain the cry of distress that had escaped her. The scream had been for nothing. Nobody had really heard her. She'd taken that as a given.

Almost twenty years later, in the huge waiting hall filled with all these voices that were overlapping, mingling, and climbing over one another, the same scream, the same overflow was about to rush out. She could feel it rising. Like a wave, a flood, an irrepressible tsunami. Like a galloping horse about to crash through a gate.

And all of a sudden, she saw her, the small, dark-haired woman sitting on one of the wooden benches, not far from the monument to the dead, dedicated to all the Palais staff who'd been killed in one or the other of the two wars. She saw her, holding her purse tight under one of her arms, while the other arm was immobilized by an electric-blue sling fastened with velcro. The tile installer's wife. The one who'd been beaten with a hammer less than forty-eight hours earlier. The one whose husband had just been sentenced to a year, six months without parole, as a result of Claire Kauffmann's summation.

She dropped her files. Papers scattered at her feet, sliding all around her on the smooth marble floor. A young lawyer in a black gown, hair smoothed down with a thick layer of gel, rushed over, kneeled down, and began picking up the papers one by one. She ignored the handsome kid, stepped on the documents, and walked to the wooden bench next to the monument to the dead. The tile installer's wife looked up at her with eyes full of tears, and one of them had a dark bruise surrounding it. While a few yards away, the lawyer was putting the pages of her summation back in order, Claire Kauffmann had a long talk with the tile installer's wife.

They ended up sitting in the middle of the constant to-ings and fro-ings, talking like two friends scarred by life, understanding each other without having to spell things out, each recognizing in the other woman an unconscious gesture, a protective attitude, an imperceptible tension in the body revealing fear at first but lessening with the progress of the conversation. In the end, they smiled at each other, and the tile installer's wife put her free hand on the young magistrate's arm. Claire Kauffmann stood up and the lawyer in the black gown, who'd been hanging around for fifteen minutes, used the opportunity to bring her her file.

"This sure is heavy. You shouldn't carry such heavy things, mademoiselle," he said, handing her the files.

She looked him straight in the eye, bestowed a charming albeit slightly awkward smile. "You're absolutely right, Maître. Would you mind very much dropping it off in the Clerk's Office? I won't be needing it anymore today."

She left the waiting hall, leaving the lawyer flabbergasted and with an armful of papers, watching her walk away at a leisurely pace, with her light footsteps.

Over the phone, Nadia had given him an appointment at eleven p.m. At first, Kern had refused—he knew that the pain in his joints wouldn't allow him to hold on till then and that he had to go back home at all costs—but she had insisted. It was eleven p.m. or nothing.

He'd found a place to wait a little farther away, at the back of a brasserie on the corner of Rue de Bruxelles and the boulevard. The waiter, this time an old veteran in a white apron and black waistcoat, had been watching him from the corner of his eye. Father Kern had been sitting there for nearly four hours, perfectly stiff and motionless in front of his empty cup of coffee, and there seemed to be no way of moving him an inch. In fact, he was overwhelmed by the pain, watching passersby on the sidewalk as though they were miles away, lost behind a kind of

damp, sticky fog that was made even thicker by nightfall. Moreover, the fever was muddling his thoughts, and it made a sickly
mixture together with the heat and the stench of fried food and
toilet freshener lingering at the back of the room.

Finally, he checked his watch and left the brasserie, while
the suspicious waiter rushed to count the coins he'd left on
the table. Once he was outside, he lit his pipe. The acrid smell
of smoke filling his mouth did him good. Once again, he
walked in the direction of Rue Blanche. The atmosphere in
the area had changed. The nocturnal fauna was claiming back
its rights, chasing away the daytime tourists, bathing in the
illumination of headlights and tacky neon signs in the windows of peep shows. At the outside tables of bars, beer was
flowing freely.

When he reached the door, he keyed in the code he already
knew by heart, and which he'd pretended to write down four
hours earlier over the phone. Before he stepped inside, he locked
glances with the dark-circled eyes of the waiter with sideburns.
He was balancing five glasses of beer on a tray. It was exactly
eleven p.m.

In the bicycle-filled courtyard, he knocked on the door and
the impact of his finger joints against the wood sent shocks of
pain through his entire forearm. "I won't be able to get through
this," he thought, "I'll never manage it."

The door opened and Nadia appeared. She crossed her arms
and looked down to study the small, stocky, intimidated, feverish man standing in front of her.

"I knew it. The guy from the cemetery. I recognized your
voice immediately when you called."

"May I come in? I'd very much like to sit down."

"Make yourself at home. It seems you already have your little habits."

She stood aside after a hesitation that was a little too well
rehearsed. Father Kern went into the studio, which was about
a hundred square feet, basic, functional, with a white tile floor
partly covered with a faded Oriental rug. On his way, he glanced
at the bathroom, the door to which had been left ajar. It was the
same shower curtain as in the picture on the Internet. It really
was Nadia whose photo he'd seen, naked and on offer in her
bathtub.

At the back of the apartment, a halogen lamp dimmed
as low as possible spread a dreary glow over a bed covered in
bright-colored cushions. The rest of the room—the table, closet,
computer, kitchen corner, bottles of alcohol, glasses, pairs of
shoes lined up in a corner—were bathed in a semidarkness that
even candles placed on the floor struggled to light. Nadia came
in and stood with her back against the wall. The fragile glow
of the night lights made her eyes shine. Seeing her against the
white surface like this, Kern thought of Luna, and her dead body
on the floor of Notre Dame, her black hair shimmering by the
light of the candles. Nadia lit a thin cigarette to hide her embar-
rassment. They observed each other like this for a while in total
silence. She'd propped up her elbow on her hip. The cigarette
burned slowly in the air, just below her face, drowning the top
of her bust in smoke.

"You were Luna's client, is that it?"

Words came to Father Kern with a kind of delay. The fever
was keeping him distant. The pain in the joints of his hands was
slowly bordering on burning, and he stuffed his hands in his
pockets in a vain attempt to quench the fire. She took a drag
from her cigarette. The incandescent tip lit her mouth with an
orange mark at which Kern stared as though it were the distant
glow of a lighthouse in the open sea.

"What do you expect me to do—take over from her? Luna

has only just been buried and you show up here to rent the other North African on duty. Is that the idea?"

He stared at her with curious intensity, as though he was struggling to grasp the meaning of her words. His eyes wandered to the windows between which she was standing. On the other side of the panes, he could see closed blinds. He would have given anything for her to throw open the windows fully and cool off the stifling room. His thoughts kept taking him back to the glass jar, in Notre Dame, where he heard the confessions of visitors. Perhaps it was because of the lack of air. Perhaps it was because of his silence, which he adopted automatically, the same way he would use silence to encourage those worshippers who had trouble confiding what was in their hearts.

"Shit, you're not very talkative, are you?" She inhaled the smoke one more time, then came away from the wall. "It's two hundred euros an hour, same as Luna. Safe sex, including oral, and no anal. Same as Luna. Don't worry, you won't be able to tell the difference in the dark. I taught her everything she knew."

She drowned her cigarette in the sink and switched off the halogen lamp with the tip of her shoe. When she turned to Father Kern again, she had unfastened her dress, and her breasts looked pointy in the light of the three remaining candles. Kern was petrified.

She came closer. Her dress slid to the floor. Perched on her heels, she towered over the small priest by at least a head. She took his hands out of his pockets, gently opened them, and placed them on her breasts. Kern was shaking. He muttered a tense "No," which she immediately smothered in a gentle interjection that stretched like a caress:

"Shhh ..." She said he looked like a beginner. Like a young teenager. She told him to relax. She told him his hands were burning hot. She asked him what he liked doing.

Father Kern had never touched a woman's body. Never like this. It was the fault of his illness, not his faith. His teenage years, before he went to the seminary, were spent in pain and isolation. Now what he was discovering about these curves, rather late in life, was causing him the utmost surprise and pulling him out of his feverish torpor. As Nadia took his hands and brought them up to her breasts, he expected to grab an ember, to touch something incandescent, inebriating like strong alcohol. Yet her breasts seemed soft and fresh, like dipping his hands in milk. This young woman's skin made him feel so peaceful that a simple caress seemed to have transformed the illness he'd been carrying around since childhood almost into a recollection that was, of course, most vivid in his memory, yet somehow outside his body.

Kern took his hands away from Nadia's chest and placed them on her waist. He laid his head on her breasts, as though attracted by a magnet to the perfume in the hollow of her neck. He could feel the young woman's heart beating in his ear, her tender flesh throbbing against his cheek, and, although he didn't immediately notice it, something within him was released. He wept. Nadia put her arms around him. He realized he hadn't cried since he was a child and, suddenly feeling as old as the world, for these few seconds that felt like an eternity, he gave himself permission to make up for lost time.

Then he straightened up, wiped his tears with the back of his hand, and whispered an almost inaudible "thank you," which, however, came from the very depths of him. Nadia's breasts were wet with Father Kern's tears. She gathered the flowery dress that formed a flower around her feet, and got dressed without saying a word. The summer fabric absorbed the salty liquid. She sat on the bed, crossed her legs, lit a cigarette, and took the time to blow out smoke before she spoke. "All right. Let's make it a hundred and fifty euros."

"Excuse me?"

"I think we'll call it a night. You look a bit tired. That'll be a hundred and fifty euros."

"I don't understand."

"Whether it's tears or sperm, you have to pay, my dear little monsieur. I did you some good, you caressed me, now you pay for my time."

"I simply came to talk to you."

"You've no idea how many old guys come here to talk, ogle, grope, but not really to screw. Whatever it may be, you still have to pay for the service."

"But I don't have that kind of money on me."

She tensed up and her tone suddenly changed. "What are you saying? What did you think you were coming to do here? Get a free coffee?"

"I'm truly sorry, I thought I was coming to talk about Luna."

"Fuck! That woman's always had a talent for picking up losers." She grabbed the cell phone she'd left at the foot of the bed. Her fingers tapped on the touch screen with disconcerting speed. Someone picked up at the other end. "It's Nadia. Gillou, I need you. I picked up one of Luna's clients. He's refusing to pay. Weird guy. Hundred and fifty." She tossed the phone on the pillow and stared at Kern calmly, her legs still crossed, her hand going to and fro from her lips in time with puffs on her cigarette. Pain was once again taking over the priest's body, this time at the speed of a tsunami. Less than twenty seconds later, he heard the courtyard door open and a man with an imposing build came into the studio. He had thick sideburns, like two triangles of carpeting. It was the waiter from the café next door.

"What's the problem, Nadia?"

"Monsieur wants to touch but not pay."

"Look, mademoiselle, I think there's been a misunderstanding."

"You're right there, and Gillou's going to straighten it out. Go easy, Gillou, he's got some kind of bone disease or something."

The man called Gillou grabbed Father Kern by the collar of his jacket. Without exercising any actual brutality, somewhat like a cattle breeder immobilizing a young calf, he jammed the short man against the wall and relieved him of his wallet. He threw it on the bed without looking at it.

"Pay yourself, sweetheart. I know him, your dwarf. He had a drink outside the café this afternoon. You don't forget a face like this. And later, I also had a cop drop by. I could smell him a mile away. He sat inside, watching what was happening on the street. There's something fishy about all this."

"I don't think there's a connection, Gillou."

"I'm telling you, there's something fishy here."

Nadia wedged the cigarette between her lips and opened the wallet. She suddenly froze. "What's this?"

The metal cross Kern usually wore on his lapel had replaced the cigarette in the young woman's fingers. "The old guys who come to see me usually shove their wedding rings in their wallets. What's this cross? You a priest or something?"

Father Kern didn't answer. The pain prevented him from thinking and his hands were shaking like two leaves. He clung to the distant, comforting image of the Bayard alarm clock in pieces on the little table in his bedroom, as though remembering the old mechanism had the ability to put him back in control of the situation as well as of his pain. Nadia closed the wallet. "It's Luna's priest, Gillou. The one she told us about. Fuck, it's pathetic. And on top of everything else, the asshole hasn't got any dough."

Gillou seized Kern by the collar again, but this time without taking the slightest precaution. "So you're Luna's priest? Can you tell us what happened in that shitty cathedral of yours? What was Luna doing there? Do you know?"

He'd now grabbed him by the throat and was calmly constricting his windpipe. Kern was nailed against the wall. He clutched at the waiter's fists but these seemed so disproportionately large, they were almost inhuman. His lungs were starting to run out of air when Nadia suddenly got up from the bed. "Let go, Gillou. This guy's made of china—he's going to drop dead on us. Anyway, it's not him that killed Luna."

"How do you know that?"

"He's a priest. An old fucker, a pervert, anything you like, but he's no killer. Just look at him. Luna would have smashed his head in a heartbeat if he'd tried to hurt her."

"And I don't believe it was that wacko they showed on TV. The one who went through the window."

"Let go of him, Gillou, let go."

"I don't believe it, I tell you."

Nadia screamed. "Fuck! Let go! He didn't do it."

"How are you so sure?"

"Because all this guy did with me was blubber."

"What?"

"He took me in his arms then started blubbering all over my breasts."

The waiter loosened his grip and Kern collapsed on the floor.

"Blubbered, you say? He blubbered over your boobs? Fuck, who is this perv?"

"Just chuck him out."

"What about your money? You want me to take him for a stroll to the ATM?"

"Chuck him out, I said. Here, give him back his stuff, give him back his shitty cross. Please, just do it, Gillou. I can't stand this anymore, I'm tired. Luna's dead. We buried her. I'm fed up with being a whore so I can have money. I want to go to bed. Sleep and not wake up again."

She was sobbing but tears refused to flow.

The waiter grabbed Kern by the belt. Not understanding how it had happened, the priest ended up sitting on the sidewalk of Rue Blanche. Finally, some fresh air—more or less. Gillou was standing over him, hands in his pockets and a cigarillo in his mouth.

Some passersby stopped and offered to call the fire brigade. The waiter indicated his café, a few yards away. "Don't worry, he's a customer. We know him well. He's been heavy on the drink again. It's like this every night. Keeps knocking it back in the bar then falls on his face on the sidewalk. I let him get some air before closing time. He'll feel better in a couple of minutes, then he can go home. I hope you didn't drive here at least, Lucien. You shouldn't drive with all you've got in your blood stream. Lucien, do you hear me?" He took a hand out of his pocket. "Here's your wallet. You left it on the counter again."

He put it into his jacket pocket. Reassured by this gesture, the onlookers walked away and Gillou lifted the priest by his collar.

"Now you get out of here, priest. Go dip your quill someplace else. And if ever you come back to bother Nadia, I'll nail you to a cross like you know who. You got me?" Then he took out Father Kern's metal cross, and threw it into the gutter.

It took him several minutes to find it. He was no longer in control of his hands or his balance. His vision was blurred. Why hadn't he stayed at home? Why had he decided to play at being an investigator? Cars brushed past him dangerously and honked

their horns. On the sidewalk opposite, a group of three young
people were going up toward Place Blanche. One of them had
a bottle of Coca-Cola wedged under his arm and his two fists
stuffed in the pockets of his tracksuit. They called Kern a drunk-
ard and made fun of him as he searched the gutter for his cross.
At the corner of the street, impassive, Gillou was bringing the
tables inside one by one.

The priest finally managed to find his cross. He held it tight
in his hand as he walked toward the square, supporting himself
against the walls in order not to collapse. He knew that if he fell
again, he wouldn't be able to get up. His joints were on fire and
his legs weren't quite obeying the orders of his brain. He looked
every bit like a thoroughly hammered drunk, except that the
only drunkenness eating away at him on this interminable Via
Dolorosa to Place Blanche was pain.

He crossed the boulevard like a blind man, his arms out-
stretched toward the cars, to the screeching of tires, the screaming of horns and drivers, putting one foot in front of the other
in a precarious balancing act, propelled by the movement itself
rather than by his own will. The world was now made up only of
blurred, multicolored lights, and anarchic voices and noises that
echoed painfully in his head. He was unable to make any order
out of them. The night had turned into a long tunnel he could
not see the end of.

He collapsed on an empty bench on the median strip. How
many times had he already walked by there in the past few hours?
He'd lost count. He kept seeing himself standing at the edge of
a grave, surrounded by young people in white, but he no longer
knew who was in the coffin, or if the memory belonged to that
day or to the day before or to his youth. He felt trapped, locked
up in that everlasting round trip between the den in Rue Blanche
and the Montmartre cemetery. He looked at his fists, which he

kept obstinately clenched. The neon signs of the sex shops gave them a violet tint. Or was it the red marks of his illness that were turning a dark purple? How would he get out of here? How would he get home? He rummaged in the pocket of his jacket. His wallet was there. This both comforted and surprised him. He couldn't remember how it had been put back there after he was searched by the waiter with sideburns. He opened it only to realize that there wasn't a single bill left. How would he get a cab? How would he get back to Poissy? How would he even walk as far as the Métro entrance he saw nearby? He remained there, sitting on the bench, distraught, his tiny cross clenched in one hand, his wallet in the other, staring at the tower of the Moulin Rouge opposite him, and at the mesmerizing movement of its luminous sails. Once again, he thought of the Bayard alarm clock. This time, he was no longer able to put the pieces together in the huge disarray of his memory.

The three young people he'd seen earlier, and who had been watching him from a neighboring bench while passing around a joint and a bottle of Coke, finally approached. One of them slumped down next to him. Later, he wouldn't remember their faces, only the smell of the one sitting next to him, a smell of whiskey and leather coming off his biker jacket, a black jacket worn despite the heat, with white letters at heart level. He would remember that smell of whiskey, which was markedly different from the smell of vodka in which he would float later, a little farther along his way through the narrow streets of Paris and his purgatory.

"Hey, daddy, you had too much to drink? Aren't you scared, all alone with your dough in your hand? Aren't you scared of thieves, daddy?"

Which of the three had spoken? At first impression, it wasn't the one next to him, who kept silent while absentmindedly swigging his bottle of whiskey and Coke. The other two, standing before him, suddenly looked disproportionately tall.

"What's the matter? Are you sick?"

"What's he saying?"

"He says he's hurting all over."

"Where does it hurt, daddy? Momo, give him a puff."

"You crazy or what?"

"Fuck, he says he's in pain. Give him a puff. Go on, daddy, have a smoke, it'll do you good."

They placed the paper cone between his lips. At first, he refused, but the second time, he inhaled and the smell immediately brought back to his mind the cells of Poissy detention center. He inhaled again, and again, and again. He was beginning to forget his body, to take off, to float in the warm air like a smoke ring. The cannabis opened up the doors of his memory, taking him back to his brother, at the very beginning, during the first years of his downward slide, before the hard drugs, before all the problems with the police, before jail.

They took the joint from his mouth. "Go easy on this, daddy, it's good stuff."

"Feeling better, daddy?"

"Do you have all you need?"

"Do you want some to take home, daddy? Doctor Momo's orders. I can give you a prescription if you like."

The others laughed. Kern did, too, not really knowing why.

"How much have you got on you?"

"Show us your dough. How much have you got there, daddy?"

"How much has he got?"

"Fuck, not a cent. What's this old son of a bitch?"

He didn't see the leather-clad elbow coming. He felt the impact with his face only later, once he was on the ground and the volley of kicks had started, and he curled up as best he could under the bench in order to bear them. It was the black jacket hitting him. The other two stood by and watched, hands in the pockets of their tracksuits. He felt warm liquid pour out of his nose, flood over his cheek, into his ear, over his neck and hair. For a few moments, his lips had been moving in vain, and nothing and nobody seemed to be granting his prayer. And he wasn't addressing God, but his brother. Finally, he heard shouting and the blows ceased.

He felt someone pull him out from under the bench. Instinctively, he shielded his head with his arms but a pair of strong hands grabbed them and pulled them away. He gave up fighting, laid himself open, his arms crossed over on the sidewalk asphalt. What could he, a four-foot-ten runt, possibly do? So he gave in to his fate, to his martyred body, to the blows, and even the prospect of death. His muscles relaxed. For a moment, he thought he was being called back to God, yet the seconds lapsed, each one lasting an eternity. When his nose finally allowed a thread of air through, and he was able to breathe, he saw that something had changed, or rather he smelled it. The odor of whiskey had been superseded by that of vodka. When he opened his eyes and looked up at the sky, he saw a big, bearlike head, large and hairy, something prehistoric, watching him, with fur that changed color to the rhythm of flickering neon signs and headlights sweeping over the median strip. He suddenly felt he was being lifted up in the air and placed on a feather comforter. He clung to it, like a child does to a huge cuddly toy, although only God knew just how much the teddy bear stank. His body was weightless, and he felt light as air. Blood was streaming out of his nose. He raised his eyes to the sky. Above him, the sails of the Moulin Rouge were still performing their lazy circular movement, a movement that nothing seemed in a position to stop that night.

⚜

He drifted. The streets of Paris, bathed in this nocturnal bustle so typical of sweltering nights, paraded before his half-closed eyes. People watched him go by with astonishment, some pointing their fingers at him, others laughing. But he knew he was now safe, shielded beneath a shell of filth and stench. Nobody would approach him again tonight. He could finally rest. He closed his eyes completely and let himself be cradled. Dried blood had formed a crust on his cheek and neck. He could hear a crackling sound at every sway of his head, at every nod, to the rhythm of the steps that were carrying him from one arrondissement to another. Steps that weren't his own.

He let his soul drift. He now saw himself dressed in white, alone on the edge of an open grave where his older brother's body had just been laid. He was seventeen and his dead brother had just turned twenty. The gravediggers were sealing the older brother's tomb forever, handing him over to the rot of time, to worms, to dust, while the younger one remained on the edge of the abyss, his whole life before him and the experience of pain already rooted deep in his memory.

Three days later, he went back to the cemetery, to bid his brother a final farewell. He'd aged thirty years. He was drained. He walked along the graveled paths. He saw the flowers from the ceremony, from the burial, already wilted. He walked closer. The slab had been upended, and the grave was open, empty, deserted. He looked around. He called out. He could see his older brother walking away among the graves. He ran after him. The tombs scrolled by, anonymous, cold, smooth. He called out again. His older brother stopped, turned around, his face as it was during adolescence, intact, as it had been when they loved each other and had been close, before the drugs, before the dependency. His older brother spoke. He said goodbye. He held him in his arms.

He told him to get on with his life. He told him to seek the light. He told him that his little body was weak but that there was also much strength in it. He finally walked away. He returned to his grave. He vanished forever beneath the earth, after one last smile filled with a youth that would never have the chance to fade.

Was Kern dreaming? To what lands in his memory had his delirium and his fever taken him? He was now going through a gate. He heard the soil crunch under his feet. There was thick foliage all around him. He could finally lie on the ground. A blanket, a bed, or something akin to it. Rest his painful, motionless limbs. Spread his arms on the cool, damp grass. Sink into unconsciousness. Where was he? Above him, the black form of Notre Dame rose against the night, like a gigantic spider with a heavy body supported by its flying buttresses. He could see the apse drawing nearer. He reached out to try to touch it. He saw a figure come away from it, and walk around it. A white, pure, female figure with silky hair. He watched as she walked up the steps, nervous and suspicious, saw her knock on the door and wait, growing impatient. The door opened, allowed her to slip in, and another form took her place in the doorway: larger, darker, that of a man whose face remained concealed in the shadows, and who took the time to give a worried look outside before closing the door and also disappearing.

At last, he closed his eyes. He could feel that he was sinking once and for all, and yet he couldn't quite fall asleep. Because of that light, distant still, shifting, immaculate, but which kept coming toward him and to which he felt irresistibly drawn.

They start walking again before dawn. They want to reach the village situated on the hill before the first rays of the sun. To seal off

the area as quickly as possible, quietly, and in the dark. Later, they won't find anything. Later, once it's daylight, it'll be too late. That's what the sergeant said last night, and the sergeant is well-respected.

By the light of their lamps, before leaving the partly dried-up wadi, they fill their flasks at the murky trickles of water flowing here and there. It's going to be a sweltering day. August here is unforgiving and you must never run out of water. It must be used sparingly. That's what the sergeant reminds the second lieutenant in a few words, as the latter is already starting on his canteen when their ascent up the ridge has barely begun.

At the end of the day, once the operation is accomplished, they'll go back to the base camp, probably by chopper, at worst by truck, and drink warm beer until their thirst is fully quenched, and think about the day to follow, about the next mission, and never mention the past. That's how the Pursuit Commandos spend their resting hours.

Halfway up the slope, there's the scheduled stop to radio in for confirmation. The orders are confirmed. To make a sweep of a village in the forbidden zone, where activity appears to have resumed. Check everyone's documents. Do some clearing up. Stop the villagers from returning to live there. And—who knows?—perhaps recover the radio they've been chasing after for days, a PRC10 they lost during an engagement, and which some conscripts said they'd already glimpsed twice, through binoculars, on the back of a Fellagha on the run. The sergeant has turned this into a personal affair. The sergeant has great respect for equipment. He doesn't like to see knowledge in the enemy's hands. The young second lieutenant knows this, and he would quite like to recover the radio and give it to the sergeant as a trophy, as a first sign of complicity. Ever since he's assumed the command of the paratroopers, the second lieutenant feels he's being sized up, judged, and sometimes disapproved of by his junior. It's the classic clash of styles between an old veteran who learned everything in Indochina, and a boy from a good family, from a long line of soldiers, fresh out of officer school. The sergeant has never taken the liberty to make a single criticism. Not once. However, his silence speaks volumes. His silence and some of his attitudes. Like the brief, practically imperceptible disgust he showed when, earlier on, the second lieutenant held out his flask to offer him a drink of water. The second lieutenant suspects it will take time to earn respect. Time, and passing the test of commanding open fire.

For now, they walk a few more minutes in almost total darkness. Their eyes have gotten accustomed to it. At times, they check with the soles of their combat boots that the stones are solid. A fall wouldn't be dangerous but it would make noise. In this setting, the smallest rolling pebble can be heard within a five-hundred-yard radius. Behind them, they sense daylight breaking. They must pick up the pace, and reach the ridge from which they'll be able to control part of the djebel. They'll leave the AA52 machine gun all set up on the top of the hill, then come back down to the right, toward the first mechtas of the village and there, in those loam houses, they'll achieve the final objective of their mission.

FRIDAY

NEVER BEFORE HAD HE SEEN THE DAWN AS A REBIRTH. PERHAPS it was because he'd slept out in the open and there was something new and unblemished about this sunrise over Île de la Cité. Perhaps it was because of the violent events of the night before. Perhaps because he'd been afraid—for his life and his body.

He let the shadows and the timid light of daybreak caress him. He was smiling like a fool and breathing through his mouth to escape the inexpressible stench he was steeped in, and which originated from the sleeping bag he was lying in. He hadn't tried to move his limbs yet. For the time being, he chose to keep them numb and anesthetized by the night. He knew that as soon as he got up to return to that massive stone building he could see on the other side of the green fence, his body would make him pay for the excess, the imprudence, the received blows, and maybe even for his sins the night before. He had caressed a woman's breasts. And brushed their soft tips with his lips.

The garden was deserted. Soon, its gates would reopen and tourists would swamp it with casual slowness. He would then have to extract himself from the sleeping bag and resume his double life as a priest and an investigator. Meanwhile, he took advantage of this strangely late waking hour. He was absent from the world, absent from himself, and that helped him regain his strength and partly come around.

He heard footsteps on the gravel. The leaves of the bush behind which he was hidden rustled and Krzysztof's hairy face peered out between two branches.

"You OK?"

"I'm OK, Krzysztof. Thank you for what you did last night."

"Last night?"

"You picked me up from the ground, didn't you? It was you, wasn't it?"

"Bouvard Clichy, yes, yes."

"What were you doing so far from your usual neighborhood?"

"Neighborhood?"

"What were you doing there?"

"*Polska Misja Katolicka.*"

"The Polish Catholic Mission, of course. And you were going home to sleep?"

"Notre Dame home, yes."

"Notre Dame home. You brought me all the way here? You carried me on your back like Saint Christopher with the baby Jesus."

"Here, yes. OK, OK."

"I think you saved my life last night, Krzysztof."

"OK, OK. No problem."

The Pole held out a stale croissant to Father Kern. "*Musi ksiądz jeść.*"

"Is this for me?"

"*Musi odzyskać siłę.*"

"Thank you, Krzysztof. What about you? Do you have food for yourself?"

His only reply was to pull out a can of cheap beer from

his pocket, knock it back in a few sips, burp loudly, and throw it against the fence that separated Square Jean-XXIII from the Notre Dame garden. Kern bit into the croissant. Krzysztof had probably obtained it from the café on the corner of Rue du Cloître. Sometimes, the woman who owned it would give him the previous day's croissants in exchange for a few hours during which the Pole promised not to beg from the patrons who sat at the outdoor tables. Kern was hungry. He even picked the crumbs off his bloodstained shirt, which made Krzysztof laugh. It was perhaps the most delicious croissant the priest had ever eaten.

"You find killer?"

"No, Krzysztof, I haven't found the killer yet."

The vagrant grew somber and withdrew into silence. Then, as though after a lengthy internal debate, he ended up partially unzipping his padded jacket and slipping his hand into the opening. He pulled out a faded color photo, protected with transparent adhesive that had turned yellow in parts. It was of a little girl of ten or twelve, wearing a white First Communion dress, with a wooden cross hanging around her small, slender neck. Next to her, with his arm around her shoulders, there was a man in a brown suit and a flower-patterned necktie, with a careful side part in his blond hair, and a blissful smile. It took Father Kern awhile to recognize the Polish vagrant in this slightly stiff, awkward-looking dad who was posing before the camera lens in his Sunday clothes, and whose smile gave his face an adolescent and—it had to be said—fundamentally happy expression. What had happened since the day when this picture had been taken? What event could have made Krzysztof stumble down this endless slippery slope until he ended up behind a bush in Square Jean-XXIII, in the 4th arrondissement in Paris? Kern knew only too well. He'd seen it so many times during the course of his priesthood. Misery needed a trigger, a separation, an illness, a family tragedy. A human being would fight for a long time before toppling over. Fate would have to attack relentlessly then, finally, deal you the deathblow.

Krzysztof stroked the photo with his tobacco-stained finger-tips. "Mine little girl. Helena."

"Where is she?"

The Pole looked at the priest, apparently not understanding, as though alien to time and space, and alien to himself. Kern repeated the question, pointing at the photo. "Where is Helena now?"

Krzysztof vaguely gestured around.

"Is she in Paris? Krzysztof, your daughter is in Paris? How old is she now? When was this picture taken?"

"I look for Helena. She leave Poland. She leave Kraków."

"When was that? How old was she when she left? You came all the way here to look for her? When did she leave Poland?"

In response to this last question, Krzysztof traced a date in the mix of sand and gravel that, every night, constituted his bed, a date which, alone, summed up the extent and duration of the man's fall: 1996.

Kern found it hard to ask the next question. Looking at the vagrant in his torn padded jacket, he thought he already knew the answer. "Did you find your daughter?"

The Pole grabbed the diminutive priest by the collar of his dry bloodstained shirt, and his breathing suddenly became noisy. He glared straight at Kern and his pale eyes grew misty. Then he muttered a few words into his beard two or three times before putting the photo back into his inside pocket. "You find killer. You find killer." He opened a second can of beer and stared at it, disgusted, before emptying it in one go.

A few yards away, a municipal employee had just unbolted the garden gate and was starting a vague tour of inspection.

Krzysztof hid farther behind the foliage. The priest laid his skinny hand on the Pole's thick forearm. "I will find him, Krzysztof. I promise. I promise, on my faith in the Blessed Virgin."

It was time to go. Kern waited for the employee responsible for public gardens to leave. When he finally made up his mind to get up, his limbs testified to his memories. It was going to be a day filled with pain. He had to muster all his willpower to start walking. His body, he could feel it, was at the end of its tether. He turned once more toward the bush where Krzysztof was crouching, sluggish, huddled in his wine-colored padded jacket that was shedding feathers, and felt a pang in his heart.

He rinsed his face at the fountain on the corner of the square and Rue d'Arcole. His head was still caked with dried blood from the night before and he plunged his neck under the water. He shook himself like a puppy and the coolness did him good. Father Kern turned to the façade of Notre Dame. The two towers rose above his dripping head and, for the first time in his life, he thought they looked menacing. It wasn't eight yet, and the Portal of Saint Anne was still shut. He'd have to go through the gate reserved for the staff, on the side of the Seine, walk along the cathedral south wall, past the presbytery, before he'd reach the sacristy door. At this time, with a bit of luck, he wouldn't meet anybody before he'd had the chance to change his clothes. He needed to get rid of his dirty clothes and of Krzysztof's smell of alcohol that permeated him. And above all, he had to cleanse himself of that moment of distraction when, as he lay his hands on a woman's skin, he forgot nearly everything.

Like a shadow, he slid into the corridor of the sacristy and walked straight to his locker where, like all the priests at the cathedral, he kept his liturgical garments and a change of clothes. With each step he took, he was aware of every limb, every muscle, every joint in his body. He felt as though he was leaving behind a gray trail of stench and guilt, which grew increasingly dense as he went deeper into the building, and its filth was a reflection of his actions. And yet that prostitute's skin, the memory of which remained intact on the palms of his hands, had seemed so pure, so soft, so white.

As he was changing his clothes, he heard a metal object fall out of his pocket and bounce on the floor. It was his cross, which he'd chosen to remove from his buttonhole the evening before, and which he'd then kept for a long time clutched in his fist while his body was being riddled with blows. He picked it up and carefully pinned it on the lapel of the clean jacket he'd just put on. He rolled the dirty clothes into a ball and crammed them at the bottom of his locker to conceal their stench.

He sat down on the wooden trunk, as he was used to doing and, for the first time since the previous day's events, took a moment to review the situation. What did he know, exactly? What had he learned? There were twenty or so narrow wooden lockers arranged along the wall opposite him, each at the disposal of a cathedral priest. And yet one of these lockers belonged to one of the regular clients of Luna Hamache, student and prostitute, whom, four days earlier, Father Kern and his sacristan had found murdered.

His mind traveled farther back, to the end of the Assumption celebrations, on the eve of the tragic discovery. He saw himself back in the same corridor, among other Notre Dame priests, all of them busy taking off their liturgical garments, like actors removing their costumes once the curtain has come down at the end of a performance. That evening, like after all large-scale celebrations or a Mass involving a large crowd, the atmosphere was composed of different ingredients: there was the stress of the event still fresh in their minds, the relief and tiredness gradually creeping into their bodies as they put their stoles away in the lockers, and schoolboy humor to signal the resumption of a certain routine. Kern recalled seeing the auxiliary bishop, Monsignor Rieux Le Molay, still in his mass garments, walk down the corridor and go out into the fresh air on the side of the Seine, his cell phone glued to his ear. He remembered Gérard putting on a pair of latex gloves and pouring detergent on a sponge cloth after the rector had spilled his cup of coffee on the sacristy rug. He tried to recall any detail, any word likely to betray unusual tension in one of the priests who were in the corridor. He went through them in his mind's eye, one by one, trying to remember the order in which they'd left, their final words before they'd exited the cathedral enclosure. He even attempted to feel in his empty hand the firmness or limpness of each handshake as they'd said goodbye.

Exhausted by this procedure, which turned out to be depressingly fruitless, Kern closed his eyes and let out a deep sigh. The mission he'd undertaken was against nature in that it forced him, the man of God, the bearer of a message of hope, to see evil everywhere, including within his Church.

"Did you fall out of bed this morning, Father Kern?"

It happened to be Gérard, coming back from the chancel after laying out the liturgical items for morning Mass. The sacristan paused in his work to stare at the diminutive priest.

"No kidding, Father, did you smash your face? One of your cheekbones is bruised."

"A minor accident. I'd rather not tell you about my evening, Gérard."

"You got into a fight in a bar in Pigalle again, didn't you, Father?"

The priest forced a smile. "You go ahead and joke about it."

"Jokes are all we've got left, Father."

"You're absolutely right. Jokes and a small portion of faith. At least I hope so."

Gérard disappeared into his sacristy then popped his head back into the corridor. "Seriously, Father, you got the time wrong. I've just looked at the timetable and you've got nothing on until midday Mass. And then confessions from two o'clock this afternoon."

"I'll wait. I'll go pray. If not, I'll go make jokes."

"You'd better go see a doctor. Meanwhile, would you like a little coffee?"

Kern followed Gérard into the sacristy. While the liquid was pouring into the cups, they heard the jingling of keys in the corridor, in time with heavy footsteps they identified immediately.

"There's a smell of coffee in here."

"Hello, Mourad. Come in and join us. Father Kern is here, too."

The guard's tall form appeared in the doorway. "Oh, dear, Father! Did you play rugby last night or what?"

"Good morning, Mourad. Is it you unlocking this morning?"

"The shop's open, Father."

Mourad hung the cathedral keys on the nail in the paneling. Then he joined the priest and the sacristan by the coffee machine. They drank in silence for a moment, then Kern, who hadn't taken his eyes off the bunch of keys, spoke again. "Gérard, do those keys open all the doors in the cathedral?"

"That's right, they open all the doors. That bunch must weigh at least six pounds."

"Including the doors that are hardly ever or even never used? Including, for argument's sake, the little door in the apse that opens onto the back garden?"

"Those keys open every single door in the cathedral, Father, including the crypt, the ambulatory, the cellars, the roof, and wherever else."

"And is this bunch of keys kept here all day?"

"In the sacristy? Yes, of course. Nobody'd go walking around with a bulk like that on his belt."

"They're kept here every day?"

"Every blessed day, Father. The guard on duty hangs them on the nail after opening up at eight a.m., like Mourad's just done. And they stay here until closing time at eight p.m."

"And after that?"

"After that? After that the guard hands the keys to the janitor, who keeps them at his place until the following morning. It's like that every day of the year."

"What about the nights when there's a screening? When the cathedral reopens after eight p.m.?"

"I leave at eight p.m., Father. What happens after that, I couldn't care less. By that time, I'm already back home eating my dinner."

Mourad, who, up to now, had been content to just stir the sugar in his coffee, took over. "On screening nights, Father, the keys make an extra return trip. The cathedral is reopened at nine-thirty p.m. and then locked up for good at ten-thirty, once everybody's gone at the end of the movie."

"So during the entire screening, the keys remain on this hook, here in the sacristy, and anybody could have access to them."

"Not just anybody. During the evening screening the whole back of the cathedral is closed: the ambulatory, the treasury, the sacristy. Only the nave remains open to the public."

"Mourad, I'm going to ask you a very direct question: Who

had access to these wretched keys during the screening of *Rejoice, Mary* last Sunday?"

Mourad took time to think. "Last Sunday? The night that girl got murdered?" He took another sip of coffee. "I can only think of one person, Father."

"Who?"

"Me."

Kern made an annoyed gesture that caused Mourad to react immediately. "Is there a problem? Is this still about this business of the rounds I allegedly forgot to do, Father?"

"No, Mourad, not at all."

"Any minute now I'm going to be accused of killing the girl the other night."

"Nobody's going to accuse you of anything, Mourad. The case has been closed. The rector has decided not to call you before the disciplinary committee. And I know you're completely innocent."

The guard was still suspicious. "Are you sure, Father? You're not also going to start imagining things, are you?"

"Yes, Mourad, I'm sure. I know you've got nothing to do with this ghastly murder and I know you've made no professional blunder. And I know it for a very simple reason."

"And can I ask you what it is, Father?"

Kern hesitated for a moment. "The reason I know you're innocent, Mourad, is that you're not a priest."

Gombrowicz was letting himself be lulled by the gentle murmur of the Mass. He hadn't sat in the chancel, where the eight o'clock Mass was taking place, but in the nave, opposite the Virgin of the Pillar. The priest's voice sounded distant and echoed slightly, as the monotonous prayers of the handful of early risers gathered around the celebrant formed a muffled cloud around him. The cathedral couldn't have been calmer.

He yawned and thought with longing of the bed he'd had to leave early in order to be at Notre Dame the moment it opened. What was he doing here, exactly? Did he still have any responsibility for this affair? After all, Number 36 had given him forced leave after young Thibault's death, two days earlier. Was it a protective measure or a way of sidelining him? He'd been questioned, he'd filed his report, then he'd gone back home, still in shock over the fall of the blond angel, still distraught, while the Police Inspection Committee was keeping Landard hanging. The better to grill him about the conditions in which he conducted his interrogations.

The day before, he couldn't help going to the funeral of the Notre Dame Madonna, attending the ceremony, watching from a distance, standing aside, and seeing who was there. Then tailing that little priest who seemed as interested in porn sites as in the Virgin Mary. Now he had no choice anymore. He had to follow the instinct that had prompted him to pick up the investigation where his superior, Landard—not to name names—had left off: a suspect's suicide and the closure of the whole case.

He was lost in the contemplation of the statue opposite him. The white of her dress was a little dirty, and the face of baby Jesus, whom his mother was carrying in her left arm, looked too grown up, too stern, and also too plump, which made Gombrowicz feel uncomfortable. And yet he couldn't help thinking that Mary was beautiful. This was mainly due to her face, where he was focused. Her tiny mouth, slim nose, large, almond-shaped eyes, and very high eyebrows gave an impression of absence, of sadness, and also of pain, as though this Virgin wished to be elsewhere. What could she have seen, to be looking away like this? What was weighing on her conscience that she dared not admit? What had they done in her house that she could not, with decency, confide in a policeman?

A slight cough next to him pulled him out of his daydream. A woman of at least seventy had sat down on the chair next to him. She was watching him on and off, furtively, staring at him with wide-open, fearful eyes, then she would suddenly turn her head away, as though facing a dangerous threat Gombrowicz was unable to locate. She wore on her head a torn straw hat, to which she'd fixed, with more or less rusty safety pins, a heap of red plastic flowers. He thought right away that he'd come across a madwoman. It was going to be a long day. He was about to get up and change seats when she grabbed his arm. She looked at him intensely, and her face lit up with a smile that was missing a few teeth. Then the smile vanished as quickly as it had appeared, and the woman began speaking in a barely audible whisper that went on forever, with her pausing only long enough to swallow her saliva and catch her breath. He had to admit it: Madame Pipi had a lot to tell.

"Sacristan to guard, sacristan to guard. Mourad, can you hear me?"

"Yes, Gérard, I'm listening."

"Where are you now?"

"By the entrance."

"Could you come and see me, please?"

"What's it about, Gérard?"

"Do you know how to operate the audiovisual control room?"

"Say that again. It's noisy here."

"Do you know how to operate the audiovisual control room?"

"The audiovisual control room? What for?"

"It's Father Kern. He'd like to see the recording of the Mass last Sunday night again. Would you be able to find it on the computers?"

"Tell Father Kern I'm on my way. I'm just going to get the Chinese group behind me to shut up and I'll be right over."

They met at the entrance to the ambulatory and together climbed the dozen or so steps that led to the control room. Mourad sat down in front of the control panel and switched on the computers, the screens, and the editing console while Father Kern took a seat next to him. From this mezzanine floor above the sacristy, it was possible to control all the automatic cameras distributed throughout the nave, and to broadcast the Sunday evening masses live. The Mass of the Assumption was no exception and Mourad, who was handling the system confidently, opened the relevant file. Father Kern watched him, filled with wonder.

"Someday, Mourad, you must tell me where you get your talent for anything related to computers."

"I've always been interested. You know, Father, it's simply a question of not letting yourself be intimidated by them. These machines are like big toys. You shouldn't be afraid to try them. The worst that can happen is that you have to switch everything off and start again. Sometimes I do the odd favor, like carry out an urgent repair during the big masses. Sometimes, the automatic cameras get jammed in the wooden cases, so I take them out and put them back in. I take them apart and put them back together again. I check if anything's come unplugged. I like this stuff. The other day, I even did some technical work for the police. It's thanks to the cameras that we caught that poor kid."

"Yes, I know, Mourad."

"You want to see last Sunday evening's Mass again, right, Father?"

"Yes."

"But weren't you there?"

"Yes, I was, but my eyes and my memory can never take the place of all these cameras fixed in the nave. They might have seen something that escaped me."

"Tell me, Father, you're not aiming for a second career as a policeman, are you?"

"A policeman? Good God, no. I'm just interested in the justice system. It's like you with computers. You mustn't be afraid of trying. You and I make the perfect team, Mourad."

The guard had started playing a long sequence that had been broadcast live five days earlier on the Catholic TV channel KTO.

"What exactly are you looking for, Father?"

"I'll let you know when I find it. Right now I have absolutely no idea."

On the screen, the large procession at the beginning of the Mass was leaving the square and entering into the cathedral, which was heaving with people. The great Notre Dame organs were rumbling like thunder, while the choir of the Music School could be heard from the chancel. In the central aisle, a string of teenagers brandishing embroidered banners were walking in front of the silver statue of the Virgin Mary, carried by the Knights of the Holy Sepulcher. There followed the long cohort of Notre Dame priests. The procession reached the podium and the fifteen clerics split at the transept crossing, at the bottom of the three steps, while the auxiliary bishop of Paris, in the absence of the Cardinal Archbishop, intoned a litany of four Hail Marys before the altar. Monsignor Rieux Le Molay evoked the memory of the French kings: "Let us renew before the statue of the Pietà, commissioned by King Louis XIII, the oath of consecration of France to the Virgin Mary, an oath made by the selfsame king on February 10th, 1638. We declared and still declare that, by accepting the most holy and glorious Virgin Mary to be the special patroness of our kingdom, we consecrate to her ourselves, our kingdom, our crown, and our subjects, and beseech her to inspire holy conduct in us, and to defend with equal dedication the kingdom from its enemies."

Father Kern was fidgeting in his chair. Sometimes, the cameras would ignore the altar and sweep across the dense crowd of worshippers. Kern studied the screen and searched again through his recollections, hoping that seeing these images would dig up fleeting impressions registered that evening during the Mass, then stored away deep in his memory. However, nothing was surfacing, nothing connected with the murder that, a few hours later, would stain the cathedral. On the monitor, the rector, Monsignor de Bracy, came to read from the Book of Revelation. It was a passage about a woman with the sun for a cloak, the moon at her feet, a crown of twelve stars on her head, pregnant and suffering birthing pains. A fiery red dragon with seven heads and ten horns was trying to snatch her child away from her as soon as he was born, in order to devour it. However, the woman finally gave birth to a male child who would become the shepherd of all the nations, and lead them with a scepter of iron.

They read one of Saint Paul's Epistles to the Corinthians, then the auxiliary bishop climbed the pulpit and read a passage from the Gospel of Saint Luke featuring Elizabeth and Mary. Then the homily began. The prelate encouraged his flock not to let their fervor weaken, and to follow Mary in their internal struggle against the modern world.

Father Kern's fidgeting increased. At the end of the sermon, the camera swept over the congregation and Mourad pointed at the corner of the screen. "Look, Father, there she is. The girl in white, sitting in the front row, off to the side, legs crossed. Do you recognize her?"

"Yes, it's her. I remember noticing her that evening. I think as we all went up to the podium one after the other, we must all have glanced at her. Of course we remembered that afternoon's incident. I was surprised to still see her there but then my attention got absorbed by the Mass."

On the screen, they were slowly moving toward Communion. The priests had gathered around their bishop, around the bronze altar, where the chalice and as many cups as there were priests to give Communion were placed. Monsignor Rieux Le Molay raised his hands and said, "Let us pray, as we offer the sacrifice of the whole Church."

Mourad was growing impatient. That day, he'd attended five masses in his role as guard. He'd also already gone through this solemn celebration of the Assumption. Besides, he could see himself on and off in the footage, standing in the south transept, making sure people were quiet, dissuading tourists from using flash photography, keeping a constant eye on the podium in the unlikely event some lunatic would decide to attack the prelate celebrating the Mass.

At last, the circle around the bishop broke up. Some of them, including Father Kern, went into the nave, each holding a cup full of hosts in his left hand, in order to give Communion to the crowd of faithful at the back, while others came down to the bottom step of the podium and let the worshippers in the front rows approach. Mourad saw himself on the screen, organizing as many lines as there were officiating priests. Monsignor Rieux Le Molay was standing in the center of the row, with four priests on his left and five on his right, including the rector, Monsignor de Bracy. Communion had started. Each celebrant would raise the host in the air, then present it to the worshipper in front of him. On their lips, Father Kern could guess the words, as though repeated ad infinitum, which he himself had uttered many times throughout his life, "The body of Christ. The body of Christ. The body of Christ."

The cameras were filming the sacrament from every angle, sometimes wide shots, sometimes in close-up, sometimes in profile, other times head-on. The rows of chairs were gradually emptying then filling up again, keeping pace with the progression before the podium.

"She doesn't seem to want to go up for Communion, Father."

"So it would seem, Mourad. She hasn't stood up yet."

The lines of worshippers were already breaking up. In some shots, you could see the priests who'd gone to the back of the nave returning to the chancel. Mass was coming to an end. Finally, she stood up in that white outfit that seemed to attract the light, and walked the few paces that separated her from the steps. The shots succeeded one another rapidly and Kern was suddenly worried that, at the fateful moment, a more distant camera would be chosen and would pick the worst possible time to focus on the Pietà, the north stained glass window, or the great organ.

"Assuming we see her take Communion, which priest do you think she's going to choose, Mourad?"

As though by miracle, the camera seemed to linger on the last communicants. Kern sat at the very edge of his seat. From where he was, the faces on the screen looked made of pink and ochre pixels. The young woman in white made her choice and went to stand at the foot of the podium. Her lips moved, then those of the priest opposite whom she was standing. Then the latter placed the host on the tip of her tongue.

Kern sank back in his chair and, for the first time for nearly an hour, looked away from the monitor. He put his hand on the guard's arm and spoke only after a long silence. "Thank you very much, Mourad. Thank you for your time."

"Don't you want to see the end, Father?"

"You can switch off the machine, Mourad. I've seen what I needed to see."

The mule watches them enter the village, as though indifferent, bored, used to the recurrent presence of armed men in camouflage uniforms, communicating in gestures or whispers. They advance between the clay walls, cautious, vigilant, submachine guns in ready position. They pop their heads through the mechtas, cast inspecting glances inside, the barrel of the gun following exactly the movement of their eyes, as though the weapon had become much more than a metal extension of their arms—an integral part of their bodies. So far, they've inspected only empty shacks: no furniture, no food, no clothes, and no people. So far, they haven't found a living soul in the village, except for the mule.

The sergeant takes it by the bridle and pulls it behind him. At first, the animal refuses to budge, not recognizing its master, resisting with the stubbornness and distrust typical of its breed the noncommissioned officer who's hoping to drag it to the bottom of the village. The sergeant has to pat its neck before the animal makes up its mind to follow with its heavy, irregular step. The sergeant, who comes from a family of stock breeders, feels respect and perhaps even love for animals, just as he does for weapons and machinery.

Now the sergeant is walking at the head of his men, the mule on his left and the second lieutenant on his right, like a kind of small-time emperor entering a conquered land in search of the first subject to enslave. It's at the bend of the sixth mechta, where the path follows a slight recess in the ground, that they find the old man sitting on his heels, a bit out of the way, in the shadow of a wall, already trying to shield himself from the sun that's still low on the horizon. The sergeant signals the rest of the paratroopers to halt, squints at the old man, and sends four soldiers to inspect the last two houses.

The sergeant goes up to the grandfather and, as the latter stands up at the soldier's approach, puts the bridle in his hand. "Is this your mule?"

The old man looks as though he doesn't understand. The sergeant turns to one of the Harkis among the paratroopers, who translates right away. The old man first hesitates then responds affirmatively.

"Is this your mule?"

The old man nods to confirm.

"What about the girl in there? Yours, too? Who's that girl? Your daughter? Your granddaughter?"

The second lieutenant follows with his eyes the gesture his sergeant has just made toward the nearest house. As the minutes lapse, the sun becomes increasingly blinding. It repaints the loam walls with a golden light, plunging the inside of the shacks into darkness in contrast. The second lieutenant crosses the distance separating him from the entrance, looks inside, and allows his eyes to get used to the half-light. He makes out the outline of a white dress with patterns, flowers perhaps, two bare feet on the earthen floor, hair tucked into a scarf that goes around the back of the neck and is tied in front, with a few black strands escaping. The girl is crouching, her face looking up at the shape of the officer outlined in the doorway. She has her hands over a dish on the ground. Her fingers are still covered in the semolina paste she's been mixing. The windowless little room smells of olive oil and sweat.

"Does your granddaughter cook well? Make cakes? Make arhlum? She makes some for all the men, right?"

The old man nods.

"Are you both from here? From the village? Is this your house, grandfather?"

The old man nods.

"You know this village is forbidden? You know you can't be here? This area is off-limits. You have to go back to the group camp, do you understand?"

The old man nods.

"Never mind, you look like a nice old man, grandpa. And you have a good mule. You have a good mule, haven't you, grandpa? A hardworking mule?"

Again, the old man nods.

"It must carry a lot. What did this good mule carry recently? Last night, for instance, what did this good mule carry last night?"

Now the old man says nothing.

"It didn't carry sacks of food by any chance? Eh, grandfather? And maybe also one or two crates of ammunition?"

The four soldiers the sergeant had sent downhill have come back up. They haven't found anything in the mechtas down there.

"You see, grandfather, a mule is for carrying stuff. And I'd quite like to know what the fuck your mule, your granddaughter, and you are doing here, if it's not sending supplies to the rebels."

The old man keeps quiet. The skin on his face has assumed the color of the soil. Over there, next to the house, the second lieutenant has just lit a cigarette. He takes a puff then lets it burn out in the air, in a position that's familiar to him, the roll of tobacco between his thumb and his index finger, his wrist resting on the butt of the automatic MAC50 pistol he wears at his belt. His eyes drift. From where he stands, he can see the sun rising over a part of the tormented landscape of the djebel. The colors, brightened by the daylight. Breathing in the first smells which had been, until now, neutralized by the coolness of the night.

He doesn't see the sergeant do it, doesn't see him turn the barrel *of his weapon. He comes back to the village, to the old man, to the string of paratroopers only when he hears the gunshot. The bang tears through the air and echoes on the nearby slopes. By the time he turns his head, the mule has already collapsed. Its front legs gave first. For a brief moment it seems to be praying, stupidly, on its knees, begging for the deathblow that isn't coming. Then its hind legs start shaking and sagging. Then, almost in slow motion, the large body rolls on its belly and turns on its side. Its hoofs are agitated by a few spasms, before the mule becomes totally still.*

The old man hasn't moved, his eyes fixed on the sergeant's boots. He stares at them with strange intensity, as though he's asking them a question, apparently unable to take his eyes off the black leather that, despite marching all night, despite walking through streams, despite gathering dust, looks polished for inspection.

The second lieutenant leaves the mechta he's been leaning against. He walks down toward the sergeant, throws his cigarette away, and tries to put some order in his thoughts before he speaks, to demonstrate authority. He barely recognizes the voice coming out of his mouth, it's so high-pitched, so alien. His body suddenly feels too large, too numb, clumsy like that of an adolescent. "Sergeant, was that really necessary?"

The sergeant doesn't even bother to turn to his superior. Rather, he seems to be trying to make eye contact with the Kabyle grandfather who still persists in staring at his boots. "It's time to move from theory to practice, lieutenant. A kind of intensive training. A course you certainly didn't attend at officer school. I suggest you watch carefully, remember everything and, especially, please let me do as I see fit. Do you understand, lieutenant? I'm offering you here a unique opportunity to learn how to fight a war."

Then, with a simple sign of his chin, he sends his ten paratroopers inside, where the old man's granddaughter is still crouching, in her white flowered dress.

Noon. It was his turn to say Mass, and yet he didn't know where to begin. Of course, he should get dressed, with Gérard's help. Put on the green cotton stole braided with gold thread, shut the closet door, walk down the sacristy corridor, go through the heavy door that opens onto the ambulatory, cross the curtain of tourists endlessly circling the stone floor like cars on a circuit, reach the podium, bow before the altar, wait for the chancel organ to finish, turn to face the scattered group of worshippers sitting on the front row chairs—during the week, the noon Mass never draws a crowd—make the sign of the cross and, with a mind filled with doubt, fear, and anger, finally say, "In the name of the Father, the Son, and the Holy Ghost."

He made the sacred gestures. He read the Gospel. He gave Communion. What was the point of all this, but a masquerade of which he himself was a part, now that he knew, now that he was aware? What should be done? In whom could he confide? In God, of course, whose presence he was trying to feel deep inside himself and in the cathedral. Perhaps never before had he felt this internal battle between—between what, exactly? Was it good versus evil? Justice versus lies? What should be done, or said, in order to serve truth and serve the Lord? If he spoke out, if he shared with anyone the still blurry secret of which he was now the keeper, his words would have unpredictable, dangerous, and terribly destructive consequences. Had he better keep quiet? In other words, join this enormous church that, barely five days after a most ghastly murder within its walls, had resumed its habits and daily routine amid the hubbub of tourists, the smell of incense, and the murmur of prayers?

Mass was already drawing to a close. He'd gone through it, bit by bit, absentmindedly, transparently, his mind elsewhere. As he always did, he turned to the pillar with the white Virgin and intoned the Salve Regina, accompanied by the chancel organ. What happened deep within him as he was staring at this stone Madonna's beautifully pure face? He would never quite be able to say, or explain, neither that evening nor later on. He simply realized that, during the course of the prayer, the battle had shifted elsewhere, outside him, outside his body. He realized that, when it came down to it, he was not the only bearer of this terrible secret, and that immediately made him feel at liberty to act.

The final note had not yet died away when he left the podium by the shortcut, through the chancel, and went into the sacristy corridor. At the end of this corridor, there was the old-fashioned telephone fixed to the wall, and he grabbed the handset. Still wearing his mass garments, he dialed the number he knew by heart from having tried it several times less than forty-eight hours earlier. He heard the tone. The phone was ringing at the other end. Right next door, in the sacristy that smelled of wax, Gérard was emptying the censer of the ashes that were still warm after Mass. The sacristan heard the priest speak softly in the corridor.

"It's Father Kern. I need to see you. It's very urgent … No, I can't talk on the phone, not here. Can you come to Notre Dame? … When? … Please come as quickly as you can, I'll be waiting."

It was like living in a padded room where the cushioning had become thicker over the days, months, and years. In spite of the regular screaming in the corridors. In spite of the noise rising from the two exercise yards, through the window equipped with bars. In spite of the sound of television sets that, night and day, broadcast porn or action movies. In spite of the sound, every morning between ten and eleven, of fists pounding the leather punching bag hanging from the ceiling of the boxing gym, a dull sound that, when it was triggered, was beneficial to body and mind. In spite of all the incessant prison sounds, silence was becoming increasingly deafening inside Djibril's head.

His last true conversation had taken place the day before, with that little priest turned investigator, who confused his faith with his incorrigible need for justice. He'd thought about this case all night, about the murdered girl shrouded in mystery, churning over all the elements in the file Father Kern had let him read. For one night, he'd escaped, fled the immutable rhythm of the wardens' rounds as they walked through the corridors and slid open the peephole in the armored door every two and a half hours as part of the suicide prevention routine.

It wasn't a big deal per se. A news item that had nothing to do with him. Something to think about while brushing his teeth at night. And yet for a few hours, this issue had represented a link with the outside world. The only one he had left. For a long time now nobody had come to see him in the Poissy prison visiting room.

The advice sought by the little priest had made a dent right in the middle of the prison walls. The immutable march of time had undergone a jolt, an accident. And this accident had triggered—he dared not utter the word—a hope. He now wanted to know. Had the little priest found the key to this problem? Had he managed to draw from the shadows the truth he valued so much?

Sitting on his bed, Djibril grabbed the remote control of the television set he rented from the prison office for twenty-nine euros a month. He flipped through the channels, checking all the one o'clock news bulletins. There was nothing new. Two mountain climbers in distress on Mont Blanc saved thanks to their cell phone. In sports news, the Olympique football club in Marseilles acquired a new player. The beach weather forecast promised sunshine on Saturday and rain on Sunday. There was no mention anywhere of the Notre Dame crime.

He switched off the television and got up to push the button on his kettle. An hour later, he was still on his bed, with a glass full of now stone-cold brown liquid in the palm of his paw. He stirred the coffee with his spoon, and let it drip at the edge of the glass, then put it in his mouth, between his tongue and his palate. "This coffee is stale," he thought. "This coffee has no more taste." Then, slowly, he pushed the spoon down his throat, putting his fingers between his teeth to help the metal stem slide farther down. He felt the spoon go down his larynx, which contracted from the pain. He rolled to the foot of his bed, his body shaking with violent jolts. He grabbed the foot of the bed to stop himself from moving and making too much noise. Already, his lungs were short of air.

He'd taken refuge in the jar, with the door shut, waiting. Soon afterward, however, the rows of chairs outside the glass confessional filled with candidates for absolution. One hour. That's how long he'd have to wait before he could share his terrible suspicion, and confide in a low voice that which would certainly not set him free, but would, he believed, be for the best. He looked at his watch. Rather than doing nothing, which would end up attracting attention, he decided—before making his own confession—to let others confess. He almost laughed at the thought of these silly sins, so insignificant in comparison to what he was about to tell. A fault that, albeit not his own but one he had to carry inside him, would be enough to fill the entire cathedral with darkness.

Finally, after granting three absolutions, he saw him through the glass, approaching among the tourists, overtaking the worshippers who were waiting their turn to off-load their trespasses. His step was a little heavier, a little more tired than usual, but he showed no hesitation when it came to pulling open the glass door that separated him from the diminutive confessor. He sat down opposite him, took out a fresh pack of cigarettes, tore off the cellophane, and lit one without saying a word. Father Kern stiffened, and the man took the time to smoke at least half of it, looking at the stained glass windows toward which the smoke was rising, then stubbed it out on the wooden table where there were, as with every time Father Kern heard confessions, a Bible and two dictionaries. "So you've conducted your little investigation, haven't you, François?"

"That's right, Monsignor. Who told you?"

The rector lowered his eyes and looked at the back of his hands. Then he pulled out a radio from inside his jacket, a model like the one Gérard, Mourad, and all the other guards wore at their belts. He placed it on the table. "The cathedral definitely has eyes, François. The cameras help it to see. But it also has ears. I've had this walkie-talkie in the presbytery for ages. People don't realize it. I can hear conversations and know everything that goes on here. Usually, it's messages of little interest. A guard calling another to point out a pretty girl. A sacristan making note of the fact that a machine has broken down, or that a concert notice is out of date. It's all so sad, so monotonous, you could weep. But earlier on, I heard through the device a rather unusual request, a request put out by the sacristan on duty: that a priest was asking a guard to show him how the panel works in the control room. That's when I realized. I realized you wanted to stick your nose in the footage of the Mass, the one on Assumption Sunday. And I knew that you, François, would see what nobody among the thousands of worshippers who were present that evening saw."

The radio crackled. As it happened, Gérard was asking Mourad to help with a jammed medal dispenser.

The rector frowned. "We really should get them repaired. I wonder what that's going to cost us? These damned machines are on their last legs." Monsignor de Bracy turned the dial of the walkie-talkie. The voices in the device diminished then stopped completely. "I think we can turn this off now. We won't be needing it for a little while." The old man remained silent, as though echoing the walkie-talkie that had just fallen quiet. "Will you hear my confession, François? One old priest to another and, I hope, one friend to another? How many years has it been since we've seen each other every summer? Will you hear what I have to say?"

Father Kern nodded.

Monsignor de Bracy let out a deep sigh, as though exhausted in advance by the confession he was about to make. "I confess before almighty God, I admit before my fellow men that I have sinned in thought, and word, and deed, and through negligence, yes, I have truly sinned." He looked like he was about to continue but suddenly hesitated. "What precisely do you know, François? What have you discovered exactly?"

Kern put his hand on the Bible and spent awhile stroking the edge with his thumb. When he'd seen the rector come into the confessional, he'd suspected that his confidences would be spontaneous in nothing but appearance. Cornered, the prelate was here to sound out the diminutive priest and discover what he knew. As for Father Kern, he was aware that the jigsaw puzzle he was trying to put together was still very incomplete. A duel was about to start between the two men of God. It was a matter of who would confess to the other first.

"Monsignor, I know that you spoke to Luna Hamache

during Mass last Sunday. You said something to her at the foot of the podium, while holding the chalice, and the words that came out of your mouth were not 'The body of Christ.' She replied before taking the host between her lips, and what she said wasn't 'Amen' either."

"And you saw that on the KTO video?"

"That's right, Monsignor."

"Yes, I admit we exchanged a few words. Wasn't I supposed to ask after her health? That girl had been attacked by a madman two hours earlier. Wasn't it my duty to—"

"That's not true, Monsignor. You spoke to her to make an appointment somewhere."

The rector's eyes darted around, as though he was looking inside himself for an escape route. "What do you mean? How do you know?"

Kern hesitated slightly, remembering the previous night, and the sin of the flesh he'd been guilty of, a high price to pay in exchange for a few scraps of useless information. He thought of Nadia's skin, of her perfume, of the tears he'd shed on her body. Who was he to judge this other priest who sat before him? Who was he in comparison to this old man who'd devoted his entire life to the Church? Hadn't he, too, in a way, succumbed to the temptation of a woman's body? Then he thought of Luna. He remembered her body lying on the cathedral floor. He remembered her funeral, her coffin laid at the bottom of the grave, her father's distress, and he immediately looked deep into the rector's eyes.

"Luna Hamache wasn't just a regular student. She was also an occasional prostitute who entertained mature clients in an apartment on Rue Blanche, a studio that a university friend— also a part-time prostitute—would lend her. You were a regular client of hers, Monsignor."

Bracy had frozen on his chair. "Me? That's absurd? Who told you—"

"Nadia, her friend and accomplice, told me everything last night. And she will repeat it to anyone who asks, including the law."

A long silence ensued, and Kern felt all of a sudden as though he had in front of him a rusty old alarm clock that wasn't ticking anymore. There was nothing else left to do but take it apart completely, and for that he was ready to lie again if necessary.

"Isn't it time you confessed to God, Monsignor? Admit to Him your faults, your doubts, and your fears?"

The rector now looked terribly old. The lines around his eyes appeared deeper and his lips were quivering slightly. Even his body, his dignified bearing, almost military stiff, appeared to weaken as time went by. "I have sinned terribly, François, I admit it. By going to see that girl I gave in to my urges, it's true. It so happened that Luna fulfilled my deepest, most hidden, and also most repressed fantasies. With age, I felt I lost my internal battle against debauchery and lust—a lifelong battle."

"What was Luna Hamache doing in the cathedral on Sunday?"

"She came to blackmail me, François. There's no other word for it. I stupidly gave an interview ten days ago. It was on the day of that outrageous attack by homosexual extremists against the sentiments expressed by the Holy Father. Do you remember, François? They tried to display a banner in the middle of Mass. Do you remember now? Naturally, they were helped by the presence of TV cameras, so they came to stage their little publicity stunt. Anyway, I had to intervene, to show myself to the media in order to bear witness and provide our version of the events. It was a bad move on my part. The report was broadcast on the evening news. I was on the air for less than ten seconds, with my name and job title at the bottom of the screen, but that's all it took. The damage was done."

"What damage, Monsignor?"

"The girl, François, the girl saw me on TV. Naturally, I hadn't told her who I was. In fact, she never asked. For her, I was a kind of grandfather, an insignificant pensioner, I'm sure like other clients of hers. The day after I'd been on television, I saw her in the cathedral, early in the morning, sitting in front of the Virgin of the Pillar. She was waiting for me in order to demand a large sum. She needed money. She wanted to quit prostitution. She threatened to reveal everything, to tell everything to the press. Can you imagine the scandal for the cathedral?"

"What did you say to her?"

"I panicked. I sent her away and told her not to bother me anymore. I said she had no proof. I threatened to call the police."

"And what did she say?"`

"Nothing. She just looked at me and left. I waited for her the following day, and the day after that, but she didn't come back."

"Until last Sunday."

"I'd convinced myself she'd given up. When I saw her walking beside the procession that day, dressed so daringly, so provocatively, I realized that she'd stop at nothing. That, sooner or later, she'd carry out her threats. You were there, you saw her, too."

"Everybody saw her, Monsignor."

"We're agreed on that. She wasn't here to honor the Virgin. She was here for me. To blackmail me. To harm me and, through me, the cathedral. I asked Mourad to move her away from the procession, but he didn't have the time to do it."

"One could say that young Thibault did it for you, right?"

"I saw him as a sign. You see, he looked like an angel, so

pure, so pale, so blond. I heard him talk to that girl, tell her to
follow the example of the Virgin, and get back her virginity. I
saw him grab her by the hair, slap her, and I thought, 'Thank
you, Mary, you have not abandoned me.'"

"Except that Luna came back for the evening Mass."

"Yes, in the front row. Her legs crossed so high, so provocatively. Don't tell me you didn't notice her, too. Every priest on
the podium ogled her. They all did at some point or other during
the Mass. During the entire service she didn't take her eyes off
me. She even dared come to take Communion, the little whore.
At that moment, I knew. I knew I had to act."

"To act, Monsignor?"

"It's true, François, you're right. It was then that I gave her an
appointment, it was during Communion. I said I had her money,
that I wanted to give it to her discreetly, later that evening. I gave
her the code to the gate in Rue du Cloître. And then ..."

"And then?"

"And then I gave her Communion. I placed the host in
her mouth. I brushed her lips with my fingers. I smelled her
perfume. I looked at the hollow of her neck. There. That's all,
François."

Monsignor de Bracy lowered his head, as a sign that he had
finished talking.

"No, that's not all, Monsignor. You must also confess what
happened afterward, what happened two hours later."

The old man appeared to search his memory, as though not
fully understanding what Father Kern was alluding to.

"You waited for Mass to finish, for the cathedral to close,
for the auxiliary bishop to leave, for the other priests to leave,
and for the sacristan to leave. Then the cathedral opened again
and the film screening started inside. However, the back of the
cathedral remained closed to the public. You were free to act.

You took the keys from the sacristy and went to the little door that leads to the garden, behind the apse. Luna turned up at the appointed time, didn't she?"

"At ten o'clock, yes. I took her to the treasury. After Mass, the silver statue of the Virgin had been put back there. The doors had been locked and I knew that the guard wouldn't do his evening rounds there. There was no risk of anybody disturbing us."

"And then? What happened then?"

"A tragedy. A ghastly accident."

"What do you mean?"

"I told her I didn't have the money. That she'd have to wait two or three more days. I was speaking off the top of my head, you understand. I didn't know what I was doing. She started to threaten me, to try and hit me, and began screaming. God, François, I beg you, believe me, I was only trying to keep her quiet. You see, on the other side of the screen, in the cathedral nave, there were thousands of people watching the movie. I put my hands over her mouth but she fought back like a woman possessed, like the devil was inside her. So I squeezed a little harder to make her quiet, then again a little harder, until she fell at my feet, unconscious. I thought I was going to die. I couldn't breathe. I'd killed her, you see, but who'd believe it had been an accident?"

"Who indeed?"

"I ran away. I panicked. I left her there, in the treasury, at the foot of the silver statue of the Virgin Mary. I went back to my apartment in the presbytery. I wept. For a long time. I prayed to the Lord. Also for a long time. Late into the night. I tried to see things clearly. Should I give myself up? Should I confess to a terrible accident in which, after all, that girl had her share of responsibility? It would mean such a scandal for the cathedral. Can you imagine that, François, it would have meant victory for the enemies of the faith. A terrible blow to Notre Dame. You do understand, François, don't you?"

"I understand very well, Monsignor."

"What I did afterwards is something I'm not proud of. I remembered the afternoon incident, the blond angel, what he'd shouted to that girl about the Blessed Virgin and virginity. So, in the middle of the night, I came back down. I went through the janitor's room without making a sound. I heard him snoring. I took the keys. I left the presbytery and went back into the treasury. She was still there, she hadn't moved. Naturally, there was no way of disposing of the body outside. In the middle of summer, on the embankment of the Seine, in the square, all around, there are young people who spend all night talking, listening to their damned music, strumming their guitars till dawn. You can never get any sleep. My only hope was to sacrifice the blond boy. Make him bear the responsibility for this death. So I took the dead girl in my arms and carried her body to the Chapel of Our Lady of the Seven Sorrows. There, I took a candle that was still burning, lifted her skirt, and did what I had to do. I gave her back her virginity with a few drops of wax. Finally, I sat her on the bench, facing the rising sun, and left her there while waiting for the cathedral to open."

"And did you think you'd get away with it, Monsignor?"

The rector seemed surprised. "But I did get away with it, François. The police were completely fooled. As for the law, it just took a phone call to the Minister for him to understand."

"For him to understand what, exactly? What did you tell him, for him to bury the case so quickly?"

"Not much, actually. I called him as soon as the body was found. He and I didn't have to spell things out. I made it clear to him that the priority was to restore calm in our cathedral. Find a culprit as soon as possible. Avoid making ripples. Put an end to the media frenzy that was sure to follow. Already, reporters were circling around the towers of Notre Dame like vultures."

"You didn't tell him anything about your own involvement?"

"Why would I have? Of course not."

"Was it he who assigned the case to Claire Kauffmann?"

"A young, inexperienced magistrate, with, in addition, a reputation for having relationship issues with men. She took on the case like a personal crusade. And then there was also a stroke of luck: Captain Landard was on duty that day. The worst cop in Paris. Less than twenty-four hours later, they'd caught their suspect. The next day, he was dead. The little whore wasn't buried yet, and the case had already been filed away."

"So the Minister contributed to a miscarriage of justice."

"Yes, but he acted in good faith, François. You and I are the only ones to know the truth. The Minister is, first and foremost, a servant of God. Serving the country must always be a secondary duty."

"You pulled it off, Monsignor. You can be pleased with yourself."

"Don't take that tone. I acted first and foremost in the interests of the cathedral. The initial mistake was mine, I admit. But who could have foreseen this abominable attempt at blackmail?"

"In other words, you consider yourself a victim."

"I wouldn't go that far. Let's just say that the most important thing has been protected: the reputation of this church. For once, the law has swayed in our favor. And the media are slowly calming down. That just leaves you, François, and I know I can count on your discretion."

"I beg your pardon, Monsignor?"

"You understand me perfectly well. You, too, are God's soldier, you and I are fighting on the same side. Now give me your absolution and let's not mention this sordid business again."

"How can you possibly expect me to keep what we've just said to each other a secret?"

"You forget where we are, François. What I've just admitted to, I have done within the frame of confession. I have confided in you in order to submit myself to God's judgment and ask His forgiveness. You are neither a magistrate nor a police officer. You're a priest—or do I need to remind you? To betray what has now become our secret would be tantamount to betraying your vows. Come on, Father, give me the absolution."

So this was what the rector had been angling for. Throughout the confession, Father Kern had naively believed that he was the one holding all the cards, when, in actual fact, that wasn't the case. From beginning to end, the prelate had maneuvered the interview, leading his confessor to an impossible choice.

"I will not grant you absolution, Monsignor, for the simple reason that you've lied to me. Your confession was not sincere, and I see no sign of contrition in it."

"Not sincere? What on earth do you mean? I've told you the exact truth. It may look dirty and immoral to you, but it's nonetheless the truth. What do you think? That it always comes pure and immaculate, bathed in a white halo? Come on, François, don't act the little saint. You've been to prisons often enough to know: the truth is not necessarily clean, and French cells are full of miscarriages of justice."

Father Kern struggled not to let himself be undermined. "I will not grant you absolution, Monsignor, because Luna Hamache's death was not an accident at all. On the contrary, your crime was premeditated."

The prelate's expression hardened and, for the first time since coming face-to-face with the rector inside the jar, Kern thought he'd made a crack in his adversary's breastplate. He did not give him time to regroup. "That night in the treasury, you didn't attack your victim simply to keep her quiet. Did she even have time to utter a word? You didn't fall prey to panic at all. On the contrary, your action had been carefully thought through during the course of the evening."

"That's absurd."

"When you went to take the keys from the sacristy, before going to meet Luna at the apse door, you took care to slip something into your pocket."

"Oh, really? What did I put in my pocket, François? Tell me exactly, since you're so clever."

"A pair of latex gloves, Monsignor. The ones the sacristan uses to polish the silver. Unluckily for you, Gérard is an inveterate moaner. He tells his woes to the entire cathedral. On Monday morning, he cursed for an hour, before Mass and the grisly discovery. You see, he couldn't find his precious box of gloves. The gloves you used to avoid leaving any marks on Luna's neck."

"This is ridiculous. You're accusing me purely and simply of murder."

"That's right, Monsignor. And you will be made to appear before a criminal court. Nearly an hour ago, I spoke on the phone to Deputy Magistrate Kauffmann. I told her I wanted to talk with her. She'll be here in a few minutes."

"You really think so, François? Do you really believe I will allow you to destroy the work of a lifetime in just a moment?" He put his hand into his jacket and pulled out a weapon, an automatic pistol that looked old and tired, and pointed it at Father Kern. "Stand up, François. Go ahead, I'll be right behind you. Very close. Don't forget that."

He slipped the revolver in his pocket and held the glass door open for the diminutive priest.

The boundary between good and evil had shifted. It was a

subtle shift of which only Kern was aware, triggered by a man,
alone among so many others who'd devoted their lives to God,
a man who'd elected to cross to the other side of the boundary,
to the side of the forces of darkness. And yet for Kern this tiny
reorientation of the boundary was a veritable earthquake. He
then remembered a conversation he'd had barely twenty-four
hours earlier, in Claire Kauffmann's office, and what the young
magistrate had said came back to him word for word. We don't
ask ourselves if a decision is moral but whether it's legal. Rector
de Bracy had just reconciled justice and religion by dipping both
in a pail of abjectness.

"Keep going, François. And don't do anything foolish."

Kern dove into himself in search of God, calling on Him,
trying to communicate with Him, redoubling his efforts at complete understanding. This time, however, the answer to his questions was self-evident and could be summarized in one simple
sentence: he was going to die.

They cut through the crowd, which was dense at that time
of day. With a slight chin nod the rector greeted a few devout
women kneeling in the nave. One of them rushed to kiss his hand
with a ceremonial bow. He proffered her his free hand. With his
other hand, he was holding the automatic pistol, wedged deep in
his pocket, pointing at Father Kern. They walked along the south
side, across the transept, past the Virgin of the Pillar, then into
the ambulatory. A few yards before the entrance to the sacristy,
by the plaque commemorating the beginning of the building of
the cathedral in the Year of Our Lord 1163, Bracy put his hand
on Kern's shoulder. "The door on the right. Open it, François."

"It'll be locked."

"It's open. I made sure of it before coming to see you."

"You've thought of everything, Monsignor."

The door opened onto a spiral staircase that led up to the

inside gallery. When they reached it, they stopped and the rector, having trouble catching his breath, leaned against the wall. "Oh, Lord, I shouldn't have smoked that cigarette earlier. After so many years of abstinence, I'm clearly too old for it."

He pulled the gun out of his pocket and signaled to Kern with the barrel to keep climbing. The staircase seemed to be twisting up endlessly toward the heights of Notre Dame. Behind him, Father Kern could hear the rector's breathing becoming hoarser and more labored with every step. At last, the stairs opened up to a narrow gallery that ran alongside the roof. Just a few yards away rose Viollet-le-Duc's spire. The place was a veritable furnace. The lead tiles had been storing the heat of the sun since early morning. Down below, Kern could see the sprawling flying buttresses spreading all around the apse and, even lower down, in the gardens and on the embankment, the tiny bodies of tourists, many of whom were looking up in order to admire the cathedral in its immensity. The two men were over a hundred and thirty feet above the ground.

"No point looking around, François. Nobody can see us. We're hidden from the visitors up in the towers by the roof. For those down there we are two dots lost in the midst of stone gargoyles. At most, they'll see your swallow dive, but then it'll be too late."

"A swallow dive? Is this the end you've planned for me, Monsignor?"

"Yes, suicide. Once again, I was inspired by the little blond angel. That boy was a veritable gift from Heaven."

"And what would be the reason for this suicide? Luna's death? Doubts triggered by the police investigation? Loss of faith? Who'd believe it?"

"Come on, François, everybody knows about your illness. Everybody knows your pain has become unbearable. On top of that, there's your brother. His prison suicide. Your power-lessness to save him from death. Yes, François, I know all that, even though you've never mentioned it. Another perk of my relationship with the Ministry. How long ago was it? Twenty, thirty years? But you can never forget, can you, François? When it comes to certain recollections, our memory stubbornly refuses to let us down. On the contrary, year after year our memory becomes more and more accurate, more precise, until it crosses the threshold of torture. God only knows I'm in a position to testify to that. You've no idea how much I sympathize, François."

"Yes, our memory. It was never a coincidence that you went to see women of North African origin, was it, Monsignor?"

"We all carry the load of our sins as best we can. For a long time I've been carrying the burden of a fundamental, original sin, that of an entire nation. A sin I've tried to bury beneath a life of respectability and prayer. But redemption is not possible. Let me tell you: what cannot be erased is the memory of the body. The body. The body never forgets."

Once again, he pointed the weapon at Father Kern.

"I will not jump, Monsignor. You'll have to shoot me, and all of Paris will hear the shot."

Bracy smiled sarcastically. He slid the magazine out of the handle of the gun before pushing it back with a click of the breech. "It's not loaded. This weapon hasn't been used for fifty years." He put the gun on the stone railing. "I took it out of a drawer. I thought I'd use it to intimidate you. Fear, François, the universal fear at the sight of a weapon. It's what determines in a second who is the slave and who the master. It's what made you climb all the way to the top of the cathedral without saying a word, without calling out to the crowd around us. I was alone and there were a thousand of you against me. Fear, I tell you. It's why you're going to do as I say and jump. The fear of death, François."

He slid a hand into his jacket pocket and pulled out an additional means of persuasion. Slowly, with the obsessive care old people sometimes have, he put on a pair of latex gloves, perhaps even the same pair he'd used to silence Luna forever. "Don't put up a fight, François. It would be pointless. I'm twice your weight. Instead, consider that, with your sacrifice, you save the Cathedral of Notre Dame from dishonor."

Then, his arms still strong despite his age, he grasped Father Kern around the waist. The diminutive priest felt himself being lifted off the ground. It was, indeed, pointless putting up a fight. In Bracy's arms he was no more than a puppet on a string. The rector was approaching to the void. His breathing had quickened once again. Father Kern closed his eyes and thought of his brother.

"Freeze! Now you're going to let go of the little priest, grandpa, and let him walk away."

It was a voice behind them. Kern felt the rector stop. He opened his eyes again and saw Lieutenant Gombrowicz in the gallery. He was holding his gun with both hands, pointing it at them. He felt the grip around his chest loosen, as though the rector's whole body, which had up to then seemed made of stone, was suddenly turning to liquid. He let himself slide to the ground. Much to his surprise, his legs agreed to carry him, and he walked the few steps that distanced him from the void and ensured his safety.

"OK, grandpa. Now you're going to put your hands in the air and let me come closer."

With his left hand, Gombrowicz produced a pair of handcuffs. Monsignor de Bracy's lips were quivering. He began to murmur. "The body ... The body ..."

Then, with the awkward movement of an old man on his last legs, he grabbed his old semi-automatic from the railing, and pointed it at the police officer. There were two instantaneous shots, causing hundreds of pigeons to take flight. Monsignor de Bracy staggered only at the second shot, as though his solid constitution had been able to take the first lead bullet but not the second. He took another step back, briefly propped himself against the parapet, and gave Father Kern a look devoid of anything. Then he swung back and disappeared down into the void.

Currently suspended in the air, he watches the tormented Kabylia landscape parade by. The Sikorsky came to pick them up and take them back to base camp. He leaves behind him a village in flames and a grandfather in tears. The sliding door of the helicopter has been left open. The noise of the blades and the engine prevents the men from talking. The turbulence caused by the rotor blows large masses of air inside. He opens his right hand above the void and pretends to catch the wind. No use. He can't get rid of the burning sensation from the pistol in the palm of his hand earlier. The rough butt, the white notch between the two joints of his index finger dug by the trigger, the shock of the bang all the way up his forearm. It all became embedded in his flesh the moment he shot. The girl is dead. He put a bullet through her head. He shot her because he could no longer bear it—not her screams but her silence. He couldn't bear seeing her there, her fingers stuck in the soil of her house, like a rag doll, her eyes staring straight up, as though dead, while the soldiers disposed of her body. He killed her to silence the soundless screaming that was coming out of her wide-open mouth. In comparison, there's something gentle and comforting about the rhythmical din of the helicopter.

He knows the sergeant is watching him from the back of the aircraft. He can feel his subordinate's eyes sliding over the nape of his neck and his back. When they get back, they'll have to agree on the report they're going to write. It'll be more or less summarized in three letters: N.T.R. Nothing To Report. At the bottom of the page, he'll apply his signature: Second Lieutenant Hugues de Bracy.

The sergeant and he will join the men. They'll drink beer. They'll talk about demobilization. They'll talk about France. They'll talk about their parents or their sisters. Those who aren't single will talk about their girlfriends and their wives back home. They'll talk of everything except what happened that very morning. Then, later in the evening, once it's dark, once their blood has been amply watered with alcohol, they'll take a walk around the back of the truck that acts as a battlefield military brothel, just to make sure they're still real soldiers, warriors, men. It's not impossible that this time, the young second lieutenant may join the rest of the troop. Just this once, aided by drunkenness, just to silence the anguish drilling through his belly and squeezing his rectum. Just this once. Use the exhausted body of a local pauper woman to soothe the anguish that's crushing him sexually. Just this once. Then there'll be night, sleep, oblivion, tomorrow. One day, these events will come to an end. One way or another, the conflict will end and he'll finally be able to return to France. Quit the uniform. Perhaps—no, certainly—such a decision will upset his father, who's a colonel in the air force. Forever keep quiet about this past, about this soiled youth as a soldier. Choose a life that will allow him to wash away the horrors of war.

For now, the helicopter is making its way inland. The second lieutenant has now brought his arm back inside, in from the turbulence and the wind. For a moment, he studies the inert hand on his thigh and then, like a First Communion candidate or an altar boy, he clasps his hands in a sign of prayer.

⚜

For the second time in a week, the cathedral had been emptied of visitors, then filled with police. This time, they were outside, too, right at the foot of the south wall, where they were about to remove the rector's lifeless body.

Inside, a diminutive priest in liturgical garments was sitting alone, lost in the immensity of the nave, among hundreds of empty chairs. Someone—Father Kern couldn't remember who exactly—had the ludicrous idea of covering him, in mid-August, with a foil blanket. He hadn't had the energy to refuse. So now, he was wrapped in a silver sheen in the growing shadow of the day that was drawing to a close. A young woman came to sit on the chair next to him. "Aren't you hot in that thing?"

"Terribly, Mademoiselle Kauffmann."

She pulled the aluminum sheet off him with motherly care. Kern barely stirred, lost in thought. "Do you believe in God?"

"No, I don't, Father. Sorry."

"Don't apologize. You know, the real boundary isn't between believers and nonbelievers, any more than it is between Christians, Jews, and Muslims. The real front line is the one that separates the doves from the hawks."

"Those who seek peace ... "

"From those who want war, that's right."

"Don't tell me this business has made your faith falter."

"How about you, Claire?"

"Me?"

"Has it made you lose faith in justice?"

She took a moment to think. "I don't know. My point of view has changed. In a way, I've taken a step toward you, Father."

"Toward me?"

"By giving you access to the file of the Notre Dame case, I broke the rules of my profession, you know. What I did was completely illegal. Illegal, but not necessarily immoral."

Father Kern couldn't suppress a smile.

"Why are you smiling?"

"I'm thinking of how our paths crossed. I nearly renounced my vows. I suppose it was the price to pay to discover the murderer's name. I also lied more than once. None of that was very moral. In other words, I've somewhat stained my cassock. And yet today, justice is none the worse for it."

It was Claire Kauffmann's turn to smile. "I think our respective faiths have been strengthened, Father, in spite of these few deviations. Or perhaps thanks to them."

"What will you do now?"

"Take a vacation. Look after myself for a while. I think I need it. I'm going to stay with a friend in Italy for a few days, near Ancona."

"Ancona? But that's by the Adriatic, isn't it?"

"Absolutely. My body is feeling a sudden urge to bathe in the sea, and I've decided to grant it that."

They said nothing for a while, savoring the silence, the seconds passing by quietly, each enjoying the soothing presence of the other.

Kern was the first to emerge from this gentle lethargy. "What about Lieutenant Gombrowicz? Is he still here?"

"Yes, in the sacristy. I think he's having a coffee. He's waiting for the three of us to have a chance to talk together."

"Have you seen him? How is he?"

"His hands are shaking. He can't stop them. He's just killed a man."

"He saved my life, you know. Without him, I'd be cooked."

"Yes, he told me."

"I'd like to see him, ask him what he was doing in the cathedral, and what made him follow the rector and me all the way up to the roof."

"He'll tell you himself. I think the lieutenant has just realized he's a good cop. If you're feeling better, we could go join
him. You also have quite a few things to tell us."

"He saved my life, you know."

"I know, Father, you just told me."

They stood up and went to the central aisle, in the large
nave. Very soon, Father Kern stopped, a look of surprise on his
face. He wiggled his fingers, rotated his wrists. Claire Kauffmann watched him. The little man seemed to be rediscovering
his body, like a baby in his cot.

"Is everything alright, Father?"

"Do you know what time it is, mademoiselle?"

"Nearly six. Why?"

"Six o'clock. Six in the evening and not the slightest pain.
How extraordinary. As though I was rid of ... " He stopped, a
funny, childlike grimace on his face, which the magistrate had
never seen. The priest started walking with a lighter step and was
now overtaking the young woman in the aisle. Behind a pillar,
he noticed an elderly lady, lonely, who looked as though she was
waiting for Mass to begin. She kept both hands on the back of
the chair in front of her, and was wearing a hat decorated with
flowers. Father Kern let out a sigh. "Mademoiselle Kauffmann,
would you tell this lady that the cathedral has been evacuated?
Otherwise, she's likely to spend the night here."

"I was the one who asked her to stay."

"You?"

"If you're still alive, it's thanks to this lady on her chair over
there."

"Thanks to Madame P–?"

"Yes, thanks to her. In a way, she knew everything from the
start."

"From the start?"

"Ten days ago, she saw Luna Hamache talking with Bracy, demanding money. She saw the rector send her away unceremoniously. She was sitting in her usual place, where she's sat for the past ten years. Nobody notices her anymore. Nobody pays attention to her. Everybody thinks she's just a crazy old woman. She's somehow part of the furnishings, of the cathedral furniture. And yet. After Luna's body was discovered, she was the only one to suspect your boss was somehow involved."

"Good God ... But why didn't she say something sooner?"

Claire Kauffmann couldn't suppress a sarcastic pout. "Father, I don't think she's ever found anyone to talk with, here. Lieutenant Gombrowicz was the only one willing to listen to her."

Kern took his head in his hands. He remembered now. The attempts the lady with the poppies had made, and his efforts to avoid her. If only he'd known ... If only he'd been a better listener ...

She was watching him from behind her pillar, sitting on her chair, her eyes perpetually anxious. He made a friendly gesture, and a wide smile immediately blossomed on the solitary old lady's face.

"Please, Father, you can speak with her later. I'd like us to go see the lieutenant now."

Kern nodded. They resumed their walk toward the sacristy. On the way, they walked past the Virgin of the Pillar, and Kern asked the young magistrate for a moment's solitude. He kneeled on the podium steps, closed his eyes, and joined his hands in prayer. His lips uttered words Claire Kauffmann could not hear from where she was standing. Father Kern looked up at the stone Madonna. Her translucent face seemed to have recovered its legendary serenity, and, in the evening light bathing the cathedral, she looked even whiter.

IF VENICE DIES BY SALVATORE SETTIS

INTERNATIONALLY RENOWNED ART HISTORIAN Salvatore Settis ignites a new debate about the Pearl of the Adriatic and cultural patrimony at large. In this fiery blend of history and cultural analysis, Settis argues that "hit-and-run" visitors are turning Venice and other landmark urban settings into shopping malls and theme parks. This is a passionate plea to secure the soul of Venice, written with consummate authority, wide-ranging erudition and élan.

A VERY RUSSIAN CHRISTMAS

THIS IS RUSSIAN CHRISTMAS CELEBRATED IN supreme pleasure and pain by the greatest of writers, from Dostoevsky and Tolstoy to Chekhov and Teffi. The dozen stories in this collection will satisfy every reader, and with their wit, humor, and tenderness, packed full of sentimental songs, footmen, whirling winds, solitary nights, snow drifts, and hopeful children, the collection proves that Nobody Does Christmas Like the Russians.

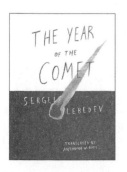

YEAR OF THE COMET BY SERGEI LEBEDEV

FROM THE CRITICALLY ACCLAIMED AUTHOR OF *Oblivion* comes *Year of the Comet*, a story of a Russian boyhood and coming of age as the Soviet Union is on the brink of collapse. Sergei Lebedev depicts a vast empire coming apart at the seams, transforming a very public moment into something tender and personal, and writes with shattering beauty and insight about childhood and the growing consciousness of a boy in the world.

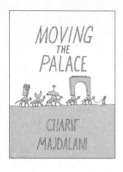

Moving the Palace
by Charif Majdalani

A young Lebanese adventurer explores the wilds of Africa, encountering an eccentric English colonel in Sudan and enlisting in his service. In this lush chronicle of far-flung adventure, the military recruit crosses paths with a compatriot who has dismantled a sumptuous palace and is transporting it across the continent on a camel caravan. This is a captivating modern-day Odyssey in the tradition of Bruce Chatwin and Paul Theroux.

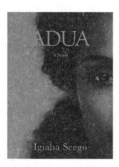

Adua by Igiaba Scego

Adua, an immigrant from Somalia to Italy, has lived in Rome for nearly forty years. She came seeking freedom from a strict father and an oppressive regime, but her dreams of film stardom ended in shame. Now that the civil war in Somalia is over, her homeland calls her. She must decide whether to return and reclaim her inheritance, but also how to take charge of her own story and build a future.

The 6:41 to Paris
by Jean-Philippe Blondel

Cécile, a stylish 47-year-old, has spent the weekend visiting her parents outside Paris. By Monday morning, she's exhausted. These trips back home are stressful and she settles into a train compartment with an empty seat beside her. But it's soon occupied by a man she recognizes as Philippe Leduc, with whom she had a passionate affair that ended in her brutal humiliation 30 years ago. In the fraught hour and a half that ensues, Cécile and Philippe hurtle towards the French capital in a psychological thriller about the pain and promise of past romance.

ON THE RUN WITH MARY
BY JONATHAN BARROW

SHINING MOMENTS OF TENDER BEAUTY PUNC-tuate this story of a youth on the run after escaping from an elite English boarding school. At London's Euston Station, the narrator meets a talking dachshund named Mary and together they're off on escapades through posh Mayfair streets and jaunts in a Rolls-Royce. But the youth soon realizes that the seemingly sweet dog is a handful; an alcoholic, nymphomaniac, drug-addicted mess who can't stay out of pubs or off the dance floor. *On the Run with Mary* mirrors the horrors and the joys of the terrible 20th century.

OBLIVION BY SERGEI LEBEDEV

IN ONE OF THE FIRST 21ST CENTURY RUSSIAN novels to probe the legacy of the Soviet prison camp system, a young man travels to the vast wastelands of the Far North to uncover the truth about a shadowy neighbor who saved his life, and whom he knows only as Grandfather II. Emerging from today's Russia, where the ills of the past are being forcefully erased from public memory, this masterful novel represents an epic literary attempt to rescue history from the brink of oblivion.

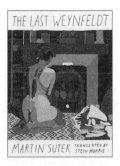

THE LAST WEYNFELDT BY MARTIN SUTER

ADRIAN WEYNFELDT IS AN ART EXPERT IN AN international auction house, a bachelor in his mid-fifties living in a grand Zurich apartment filled with costly paintings and antiques. Always correct and well-mannered, he's given up on love until one night—entirely out of charac-ter for him—Weynfeldt decides to take home a ravishing but unaccountable young woman and gets embroiled in an art forgery scheme that threatens his buttoned up existence. This refined page-turner moves behind elegant bourgeois facades into darker recesses of the heart.

The Last Supper by Klaus Wivel

Alarmed by the oppression of 7.5 million Christians in the Middle East, journalist Klaus Wivel traveled to Iraq, Lebanon, Egypt, and the Palestinian territories to learn about their fate. He found a minority under threat of death and humiliation, desperate in the face of rising Islamic extremism and without hope their situation will improve. An unsettling account of a severely beleaguered religious group living, so it seems, on borrowed time. Wivel asks, Why have we not done more to protect these people?

Guys Like Me by Dominique Fabre

Dominique Fabre, born in Paris and a life-long resident of the city, exposes the shadowy, anonymous lives of many who inhabit the French capital. In this quiet, subdued tale, a middle-aged office worker, divorced and alienated from his only son, meets up with two childhood friends who are similarly adrift. He's looking for a second act to his mournful life, seeking the harbor of love and a true connection with his son. Set in palpably real Paris streets that feel miles away from the City of Light, a stirring novel of regret and absence, yet not without a glimmer of hope.

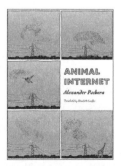

Animal Internet by Alexander Pschera

Some 50,000 creatures around the globe—including whales, leopards, flamingoes, bats and snails—are being equipped with digital tracking devices. The data gathered and studied by major scientific institutes about their behavior will warn us about tsunamis, earthquakes and volcanic eruptions, but also radically transform our relationship to the natural world. Contrary to pessimistic fears, author Alexander Pschera sees the Internet as creating a historic opportunity for a new dialogue between man and nature.

Killing Auntie by **Andrzej Bursa**

A young university student named Jurek, with no particular ambitions or talents, finds himself with nothing to do. After his doting aunt asks the young man to perform a small chore, he decides to kill her for no good reason other than, perhaps, boredom. This short comedic masterpiece combines elements of Dostoevsky, Sartre, Kafka, and Heller, coming together to produce an unforgettable tale of murder and—just maybe—redemption.

I Called Him Necktie by **Milena Michiko Flašar**

Twenty-year-old Taguchi Hiro has spent the last two years of his life living as a hikikomori—a shut-in who never leaves his room and has no human interaction—in his parents' home in Tokyo. As Hiro tentatively decides to reenter the world, he spends his days observing life from a park bench. Gradually he makes friends with Ohara Tetsu, a salaryman who has lost his job. The two discover in their sadness a common bond. This beautiful novel is moving, unforgettable, and full of surprises.

Who is Martha? by **Marjana Gaponenko**

In this rollicking novel, 96-year-old ornithologist Luka Levadski foregoes treatment for lung cancer and moves from Ukraine to Vienna to make a grand exit in a luxury suite at the Hotel Imperial. He reflects on his past while indulging in Viennese cakes and savoring music in a gilded concert hall. Levadski was born in 1914, the same year that Martha—the last of the now-extinct passenger pigeons—died. Levadski himself has an acute sense of being the last of a species. This gloriously written tale mixes piquant wit with lofty musings about life, friendship, aging and death.

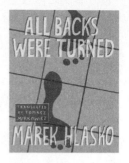

ALL BACKS WERE TURNED BY MAREK HLASKO

TWO DESPERATE FRIENDS—ON THE EDGE OF the law—travel to the southern Israeli city of Eilat to find work. There, Dov Ben Dov, the handsome native Israeli with a reputation for causing trouble, and Israel, his sidekick, stay with Ben Dov's younger brother, Little Dov, who has enough trouble of his own. Local toughs are encroaching on Little Dov's business, and he enlists his older brother to drive them away. It doesn't help that a beautiful German widow is rooming next door. A story of passion, deception, violence, and betrayal, conveyed in hard-boiled prose reminiscent of Hammett and Chandler.

ALEXANDRIAN SUMMER BY YITZHAK GORMEZANO GOREN

THIS IS THE STORY OF TWO JEWISH FAMILIES living their frenzied last days in the doomed cosmopolitan social whirl of Alexandria just before fleeing Egypt for Israel in 1951. The conventions of the Egyptian upper-middle class are laid bare in this dazzling novel, which exposes sexual hypocrisies and portrays a vanished polyglot world of horse racing, seaside promenades and nightclubs.

COCAINE BY PITIGRILLI

PARIS IN THE 1920S—DIZZY AND DECADENT. Where a young man can make a fortune with his wits ... unless he is led into temptation. Cocaine's dandified hero Tito Arnaudi invents lurid scandals and gruesome deaths, and sells these stories to the newspapers. But his own life becomes even more outrageous when he acquires three demanding mistresses. Elegant, witty and wicked, Pitigrilli's classic novel was first published in Italian in 1921 and retains its venom even today.

KILLING THE SECOND DOG
BY MAREK HLASKO

TWO DOWN-AND-OUT POLISH CON MEN LIVING in Israel in the 1950s scam an American widow visiting the country. Robert, who masterminds the scheme, and Jacob, who acts it out, are tough, desperate men, exiled from their native land and adrift in the hot, nasty underworld of Tel Aviv. Robert arranges for Jacob to run into the widow who has enough trouble with her young son to keep her occupied all day. What follows is a story of romance, deception, cruelty and shame. Hlasko's writing combines brutal realism with smoky, hard-boiled dialogue, in a bleak world where violence is the norm and love is often only an act.

FANNY VON ARNSTEIN: DAUGHTER OF THE ENLIGHTENMENT BY HILDE SPIEL

IN 1776 FANNY VON ARNSTEIN, THE DAUGH-ter of the Jewish master of the royal mint in Berlin, came to Vienna as an 18-year-old bride. She married a financier to the Austro-Hungarian imperial court, and hosted an ever more splendid salon which attracted luminaries of the day. Spiel's elegantly written and carefully researched biography provides a vivid portrait of a passionate woman who advocated for the rights of Jews, and illuminates a central era in European cultural and social history.

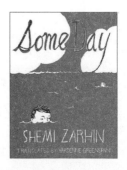

SOME DAY BY SHEMI ZARHIN

ON THE SHORES OF ISRAEL'S SEA OF GALILEE lies the city of Tiberias, a place bursting with sexuality and longing for love. The air is saturated with smells of cooking and passion. *Some Day* is a gripping family saga, a sensual and emotional feast that plays out over decades. This is an enchanting tale about tragic fates that disrupt families and break our hearts. Zarhin's hypnotic writing renders a painfully delicious vision of individual lives behind Israel's larger national story.

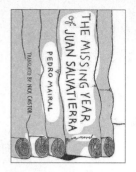

THE MISSING YEAR OF JUAN SALVATIERRA
BY PEDRO MAIRAL

AT THE AGE OF NINE, JUAN SALVATIERRA became mute following a horse riding accident. At twenty, he began secretly painting a series of canvases on which he detailed six decades of life in his village on Argentina's frontier with Uruguay. After his death, his sons return to deal with their inheritance: a shed packed with rolls over two miles long. But an essential roll is missing. A search ensues that illuminates links between art and life, with past family secrets casting their shadows on the present.

THE GOOD LIFE ELSEWHERE
BY VLADIMIR LORCHENKOV

THE VERY FUNNY—AND VERY SAD—STORY OF A group of villagers and their tragicomic efforts to emigrate from Europe's most impoverished nation to Italy for work. An Orthodox priest is deserted by his wife for an art-dealing atheist; a mechanic redesigns his tractor for travel by air and sea; and thousands of villagers take to the road on a modern-day religious crusade to make it to the Italian Promised Land. A country where 25 percent of its population works abroad, remittances make up nearly 40 percent of GDP, and alcohol consumption per capita is the world's highest – Moldova surely has its problems. But, as Lorchenkov vividly shows, it's also a country whose residents don't give up easily.

 New Vessel Press

To purchase these titles and for more information
please visit newvesselpress.com.